A Bag of Souls

PEACH BERRY

FIRST EDITION

All characters and events in this publication, other than those clearly in the public domain, are fictitious and any resemblance to real persons, living or dead, is purely coincidental.

All rights reserved.

GREEN CAT BOOKS

www.green-cat.co/books

CONTENTS

ACKNOWLEDGMENTS

To Daisy May – If you can dream it, you can do it

This book would not have been possible if it weren't for the continued
support of my friends and family, thank you for believing in me.
I would like to dedicate this book to my Mum, Jill Berry, my biggest and
most unwavering fan, thank you for everything you do!
To Lisa, my publisher, who has worked tirelessly to bring my dreams
into reality.
Thank you the incredible minds of Stephen King, James Herbert, Anne
Rice, Trent Reznor, Corey Taylor and Marilyn Manson, who continue to
inspire my own, macabre and warped brain to this day.

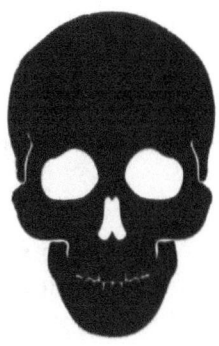

THE HOUSE OF SCREAMING SKULLS

Derbyshire, 1885

There was nothing but the silence that crept along the hallways of Bramley Lodge, to keep her company in the midst of a quiet morning, when even the birds ceased to tweet their morning song. She found it somewhat comforting to be alone with just her thoughts for company, a familiar scenario of late. The faintest glimmer of sunlight streamed through the thin bedroom curtains as another restless early rise began its relentless intrusion.

She closed the bedroom door behind her, careful to lift and replace the latch, so as to not make any sound, so as to not disturb him and made her way along the hallway to the room at the end; a quaint room with a corner desk and a pile of boxes that she had yet to sift through.

She pulled the curtains across to let the dawn light in a little. She looked around her at the stacks of books that spilled onto the wooden flooring and old framed pictures that were half-visible beneath muslin cloth. She had lived here for weeks already and yet it still did not feel like her home. The only thing in the tiny room that had lain, almost forgotten,

1

before her arrival, was the old corner desk that she had placed in the middle of the room, pointing towards the window and away from the rest of Bramley and its acres of unchartered territory.

She sat down, smoothing the faint creases of her nightdress as she sat; the gossamer-thin white cottons billowed out at across her legs, as her body gave an unwelcome shiver against the brisk chill of the new day.

It had already been too long, she thought to herself, as she stroked the metal nib of her writing pen and dipped it in the inkwell. Staring at the crisp whiteness of an untouched leaf of paper, she began to write.

18th June 1885

Dearest Elizabeth,

I send my sincere apologies for the lack of contact these past few weeks, I sit here now with my pen hovering over the paper, gushing with stories to tell you and not quite knowing where to begin. Marriage, as it happens, can be quite troublesome when it comes to finding time for oneself and one's sister. But I do miss you, you must know that, before I divulge anything else of my new life as a married woman.

James and I have settled into his home quite well; I cannot wait for you to visit us, when you have time. Bramley Lodge looked quite imposing from the distance as we wound along its narrow, winding lane, for the first time, but it is slowly becoming more familiar, as is my new life, as Mrs James Stead. I am finding my way around its peculiar little nooks and crannies and I have the whole summer to explore the acres of green that surround us. I suppose there are times when I might feel isolated, coming from the city as I do. I have gone these past two weeks without seeing so much as another soul, though I dare say there will be enough work for me to do around the house. James inherited the family home almost five years ago. He moved in just after his doctoral appointment in the village, though we are situated a good ten miles away, nestled into the countryside, overlooking the brightest hues of greens and yellows. I jest that the house needs a woman's touch; I have an eye for décor, so I suppose I may have a lot to do in the coming months.

Most days since my move to Bramley, I have had little inclination to unpack the remaining boxes and chests which I brought with me. I find the house itself far too interesting, though I do like to make the most of my surroundings and take a walk almost daily. There seems to be so much to see when you are residing in a part of the world so vast and wild, it seems almost criminal to stay cooped up in the Lodge, even when it is raining. James scolded me last week upon my return from a refreshing jaunt in the rain; my boots were almost soaked through from the long, rambling grass. I imagine most places would seem wild in comparison to the narrow townhouses and busy streets that we wandered when we were girls. Am I a woman now? I scarcely feel more than a young teenager in love, at times.

James went back to his duties a few days after the move, barely two weeks after our marriage ceremony.

We had a wonderful time visiting James' aunt in London, I think I had somewhat hoped for the glorious haze of our wedding day to last long into our marriage, but that is not what marriage is about. Day to day, I wave James off and welcome him home before I've barely started on any chores. We have two wonderful maids who cook and clean as and when we require, but I have always been the type to get my hands dirty where necessary, which is beyond James' comprehension. I must not grumble; he is a kind and hardworking man, we are happy and will continue to be happy here.

On the days that I can no longer force myself to trudge along the Derbyshire hillsides, I explore the long corridors of the lodge, familiarising myself with its winding staircases and hidden cupboards, taking stock of everything stacked in the cosy little kitchen at the back of the house. Sometimes I sit and read in the front room, which houses huge, wonderful bay windows that look out onto our rolling front garden. Whoever built this house was clearly not enamoured with cooking, but we make do with what we have and I am sure it will suit us just fine when we have a family of our own. Before you ask, I do not know when that will be. James is determined to establish himself in his job a little more, first. He works hard with the community, many of whom have taken an instant liking to him. He just seems dissatisfied, so often, as if there is always more he can do. I can hardly complain that he is a hard worker, it is a quality I most admire in him; he reminds me of our Father.

The morning is young and so I must sign off, for now, dear sister. Soon enough, autumn will rear its colourful head and the long nights will begin to claw their way in again. It will be then that I will miss our evenings together so much more. I shall have nobody to read ghost stories to when the moon hovers above us, to tell all my secrets to.

Though I do admit, sleep is beginning to evade me. Perhaps it is because I am still adjusting to my new life at Bramley, but I find myself tossing and turning at night, whilst James rests so deep in sleep next to me. Thoughts and echoes turn over in my mind and when I do finally find peace behind my eyelids, I dream of a dark shape, in our house: a woman, I presume, dressed in crisp white, faceless from my memory, drifting along the corridors and stopping at each door, as if to watch over us in our slumber. As I wrestled with my tiredness night after night, my first thought was that she may have been an Angel, someone beautiful and slight, a bringer of good feelings and peace. But I could not imagine an angel, a being of such light and such hope, would be the bearer of such a terrifying scream as hers.

Take care my sister; I await your reply with an eager heart

May

* * *

That noise again.

She sat bolt upright, pulling the bedcovers close to her chest, her eyes adjusting to the darkness around her. Still sliding between waking and dreaming, it was as if the house itself had echoed the inhuman scream, that had begun to haunt her, as if the scream itself had clawed its way from her subconscious, its echoes edged between what was real and what she had imagined. She wrapped her arms around her shoulders, clutching at the bedcovers and blankets for warmth. Her skin felt clammy to the touch. Perhaps she had been too hot, writhing in layers underneath the eiderdown, or had she been chilled to the very bone?

James slept in his own chamber that evening, after a late evening working. She lit the oil lamp next to her bed and edged her toes out from under the bedcovers, to reach the floor. She did not know what time it was, though the familiar pale sunlight had begun to creep through the windows again. She calmed her breath, as she reached for a blanket, something to place over her shoulders and she tiptoed across to her bedroom door.

The lamp flickered, off-setting erratic motions of giant shadows on the study walls, as she settled into her desk chair again and drew the pen. The little window let the light in as usual, a stillness that hung over her and the house, as she allowed her heart to settle a little, and her mind to overcome her fears. There was no such thing as ghosts.

She must not let on.

And so, she began to write, another fresh leaf of paper, another letter, a reply to the sister she so desperately missed.

14th July 1885

Dearest Elizabeth,

I was thrilled at your hasty reply to my last letter. It sounds as if you are so busy from one week to the next, you must barely have found time to read my letter, let alone reply. Reading your kind and reassuring words only strengthened my longing for us to meet again, for you to visit James and I, before the summer is over. I wonder when we shall meet again? Please say it will be soon?

Since I last wrote, time to unpack my final trunks and treasures has been few and far between. James has been working to an almost constant timetable for the past three weeks, barely stopping to eat supper, whilst he extends his duties in the village. Just last Wednesday, when he was called out in the early hours to an ailing gentleman who insisted that Dr Stead were at his side, I was both proud and envious that his patients will always be his number one priority. We are less than two months into our marriage and our life together at Bramley, and yet I do so feel alone much of the time. James is such a kind man, he must be in order to undertake such a strenuous job, one that takes so much of him. He does so much for his patients. But the pangs of some kind of mad envy do have a tendency to rear their ugly heads, when my husband is called out at all hours of the night or returns home from work late, too tired for conversation. Do you think me wicked, sister? Or selfish? Perhaps I am both, but I feel as if the stone walls of Bramley Lodge itself offer more companionship at the moment.

Listen to me; I should not be writing in such a sombre tone, I know how you will worry when you read this, I do not mean to be such a burden, sister dearest. Most days I am quite content, I am stoic and happy in my decision to marry James and all that I may deem as his faults. But there are some days that have been harder to bear, when loneliness consumes me, until the inky black of night seeps its way into the rooms in which I wander. Then I have your letters and our memories and I can find solace in those, even if they are nothing more than memories now.

In truth, dear sister, your letter has made me miss you so much more than I can articulate in these letters. You feel so far away, or perhaps it is me that feels so far away from everything and everyone I know and love. Do you remember that pale pink petticoat we fought over once? Such a strange memory to evoke, but I found a very similar one lurking at the back of my closet last night and I could not help but snigger as I remembered our petulant shouts and gasps as the silk material near enough split in two. I crave those times again, even if just for a moment, even if we were bickering and shouting at each other, then helping each other with hair rags and powders in the blink of an eye. We squabbled, but my love for you is most irreplaceable; I know that now that you are no longer within arm's reach.

Is it fair to call Bramley Lodge a strange place? In many ways, I am still settling into the high beams and turrets of this great home. Bramley stands so tall and white, against the moss and the dewy greens of the countryside, it still looks regal upon approach. Perhaps I still find it all overwhelming, as if I am being shaped in to a life that should not be mine; filling the space of a person much more deserved than I.

I think I have discovered just about all there is to discover, wandered along each hallway and sat in each room. I love the dining room, with its huge bay windows that capture the sunlight in bright, hopeful rays. I often sit in the dining room and read, basking in the glow of the last days of September, beaming through the windows in ripples across my pages. There is something so exquisite and peaceful about the dining room, the room that captures all the light.

The only place I have refused to venture is the cellar, an untouched room that, by all accounts, houses nothing but out of work brooms and old wine bottles. I often dare myself to venture down there, much like the woods we used to run through when we were children. How we would scare ourselves stupid with tales of those dense clusters of trees and the shadows that lurked within them. I imagine the cellar to be nothing more than a dingy square, thick with dust and neglect, but paranoia always gets the better of me; a fleeting shadow somewhere in the corner of my eye, a knock, a creak of a floorboard and I am drawn away, not convinced that my mind can rationalise. I know I sound ridiculous, but never more than during my stay at Bramley Lodge, have I become so convinced that there are things that exist, that the human mind, or even the human eye, cannot comprehend.

You will remember me mentioning my dream in my last letter, my recurring dream of a woman in white, a faceless spirit who roamed the halls of Bramley Lodge. I apologise for signing off on such a strange and obscure note, but I was not sure that my dreams were of any importance, not at the time. She was an angel, perhaps, a screaming angel who was sent to take care of us as we lulled in our slumber, or so I thought. Well, it was not long after I sent my first correspondence to you, that I was awoken in the night, I am still unsure what time it was; it could well have been the very early hours of the morning. I was lost in the midst of a peaceful sleep, aware of James' body leaning into mine as we huddled against an inexplicable chill that blew through the top rooms, when a very loud, crystal clear scream brought me to my senses. It seemed to start from the back of my mind but, I could hear the echo all around me. I sat up, shivering with fright and with cold, as James continued to sleep, seemingly undisturbed by the noise of our unwanted guest. The scream itself was enough to curdle the blood of even the strongest man. It sounded human, a wailing human, animalistic and raw, a guttural noise that stemmed from the depths of its spectral lungs. Still, James did not stir whilst I sat, afraid to move, only twisting my fingers an inch or so to pull the bedcovers closer to me. Within minutes, the sound had dissipated. As if cut off, there were no lingering echoes, nor sounds of anybody escaping. I could hear no disturbances in the yard or the gardens, though I *felt too afraid to go to the window and check for the possible shadow of an intruder. I lost sleep for most of that night, allowing myself to lie down, pressing my body into the small of James' back, desiring nothing but the warmth and security of his presence. I have spoken nothing of these hideous screams to him these past three weeks, nor of the dreams of our female intruder. I dare not worry him, though I must admit, I have had the same experience three times more since that night. And each night that I sit and wait for the scream to stop, it seems closer; no longer a howl from the grounds, but as if it is emanating from the depths of Bramley itself. And each time it disappears, I still cannot bring myself to move from our bed, or seek out the entity to whom this scream belongs.*

Forgive me sister, I do not wish to alarm you, but my experiences have been so out of the ordinary, that I cannot write to you with my news and leave such strange happenings untold. By day, I am able to cope with it, fathom that I may be hearing nothing more than a wild animal, roaming around the Lodge. But it is by night, when the moon is at its highest, that I feel at my most trapped, my most vulnerable, whilst my husband sleeps in such peace, beside me.

Write soon, sister; I wait for your response, even more for news that you may be able to visit.

May

* * *

Autumn had begun to creep its way across the Derbyshire countryside. The brightness of the hills that surrounded Bramley had dulled with the streams of drizzle and dishwater clouds that hung low in the sky. The patches of red, pink and violet flowers that had bloomed in the gardens through the summer were beginning to shrivel, to droop at their edges and bow under the dense sky; just as the trees, with their shedding leaves stooped and surrendered to the coming cold.

She came home from another walk, her skirt tinged with the dewy dampness of the morning. Her coat was covered in droplets of rain; rain that dropped in thin, wispy sheets, but soaked through to the skin. She had become accustomed to her morning walks in the summer, the onslaught of the duller seasons had ceased to halt her morning regime.

5th September, 1885

My Dearest Elizabeth,

I know how busy Mother must keep you with her list of demands and ever-growing need for cures for her ailments, but I wait with an anxious mind for news from home, something familiar. Above all, I wonder how you are. I do hope you will not show her this letter. I write to Mother often, as often as I write to you, though there are things I do not press her with; things that would worry Mother far more than a woman of her age should be worried. I hope my secrets can be trusted with you, sister. Why should I doubt you? I know you will not tell.

I am reminded of the evening I caught you sneaking out of the house to meet with Tom Richards; how I near enough screamed the place down with anger, as you tore down the stairs and slammed the front door, as determined as you always had been. I was so envious of you that night, Elizabeth. I was just a girl, almost five years your junior, but I remember every inch of you, a shadow in the pale moonlight, a delightful wisp of silk and curls. It was my coming of age, in many ways, it was the first time that I realised our lives would never be quite the same, now that there were tales of romance, of growing up, hanging in the air around us; that the twists and turns that would drive us, with all too much haste, to adulthood, would take us on separate paths, away from shared bedrooms and study, away from each other. I miss you so very much.

Bramley Lodge continues to be a thing of great beauty and complexity. I am not reacting to the seasonal changes so well; the draughts are beginning to funnel through the house, as if each nook and cranny of the lodge should be checked for holes and filled. That was the beauty of our townhouse; lots of bricks, piled together, for warmth. I can scarcely believe October is around the corner; James refuses to put our fires to good use, it seems, until we have snow on the ground. Still, I suppose one more layer here, another blanket there, will do no harm.

I have good news also though, dear sister, as James is spending more evenings at home. For four days in a row, just this past week, he has been prompt and home in time for supper with me by five-thirty. I had barely uttered a word about my discontent with the situation to him, preferring, as I so often do, to soldier on in the hope that things will get better. I must have seemed so miserable the last time I wrote. I think one always has an idea of marriage, of what it will bring and how one pictures their life spent with the man they love and, I suppose, I had experienced so little of that in the first few months. But we are as we are, Dr and Mrs Stead. We talk and we share jokes; we read together, we enjoy the time we spend together and it is as if the first spark of our love has flamed again for us. I know you will be happy to read this, dear sister, and I hope to see you very soon; for Christmas, at the very latest, if we cannot arrange something sooner.

My night-time experiences had ceased too for a short while, at least. You remember me, in my last letter, describing the dreadful screams that I kept hearing, in my last letter? They were scaring me half to death when, one night, James was awoken by them too. A piercing scream, that rose through the floors of the house as if Bramley itself was turning on us. James awoke but did not seem so shocked as I which, on reflection, seemed a little strange. He turned over to face me, half asleep, rubbing one eye and reaching out his arm towards me. He did not speak, yet offered comfort in his arms alone. I was dazed, frightened as the sound - now long gone - travelled through my skull in thick waves. I clutched at James' hand and pulled myself into him, protecting myself from the unseen banshee. We said nothing more that night. We found sleep again, eventually, wrapped in each other's arms and, from that day onwards, James has softened, a silent acknowledgement of those strange occurrences. And for that, I am truly grateful to feel so close to him. This is what marriage should be, so I believe. And so my sleep became a little peaceful, once more.

That was until the moaning began.

Alas, dear sister, for the calming waters of our renewed relationship are once again turbulent. There is a brewing storm with which I fear I am in battle alone, again. I am unsure whether to fight it.

The night after James and I heard the violent screaming of our inhuman visitor, I awoke one night to a faint mumbling sound. It was not the piercing screams that had so shaken me from my dreams before; more a caressing, sombre moan that drifted to my ears and coaxed me awake, like the soft prod of a finger.

I opened my eyes. My ears adjusted to the sounds, the intricacies of each syllable, that seemed to be coming from inside the room, I could make out the faint markings of a name, a woman's name, coming from the dreaming tongue of my husband. The hairs stood bristled on the back of my neck.

'Caroline.'

Caroline. Caroline, I thought, my fingers curling around themselves in agitation as I sought to find a memory of a 'Caroline', but to no avail. From my recollection of our short courtship, our marriage, James had never mentioned Caroline. The hour felt early, too early, to keep muttering questions to myself, but still James' murmurs continued in the confines of his subconscious, muffled only by the bedclothes as they fell across his face.

That was three nights ago. I have now endured three nights of these adulterous whispers, preferring to ignore them by day, to continue life at Bramley as if there is no third entity hanging over us, existing in nothing more than unspoken thoughts; a sudden gust of paranoia that grips with violence for just moments but leaves its trace in the walls, in the wind that sweeps past you, in the endless hours of silence where thoughts can so takeover.

I have tried to push the thoughts away. I do not even want to entertain the idea that my wonderful husband could be having an affair. I know you must think me mad, dreams are such secrets, such nonsense, after all. But, with all that has left me feeling unsettled of late, I cannot help but wonder if James' midnight admissions are something I should pay attention to. After all, if dreams are nothing but girlish nonsense, then I must have been daydreaming when I caught a glimpse of a woman passing down the hallway as I stepped in from my morning walk, just this morning.

A tall figure, dressed in white, who seemed not to walk, but to float her way through the kitchen and, I presume, exit through the back door. I was frozen to the spot; I felt nothing but ice cold running through my spine, the hairs on my arms standing on end. Her features were blurred; she had a mass of long, wild, *ebony hair, that cascaded down her back, floating with her as she moved through the house, a house that did not belong to her. And in the last moment, before she vanished from sight, she placed a hand on the doorframe of the kitchen and turned to look at me, or through me, but I shall never forget the twisted face, the black holes of her eyes, the mouth widening into a deafening scream that shook Bramley at its very core, knocking me sideways into the coat stand. When I came to my senses, all trace of this ethereal stranger, had gone.*

Sister, I am so eager to hear your thoughts. I have become terrified in my own home, terrified of my own thoughts. Could it be that I am losing my mind? Please write back when you can, I am eager to hear your familiar reassurance.

Sending love and wishes, always,

May.

* * *

The slam of the front door shook the house, as James sped away to work, leaving her alone, again. He had been angry when he left the house; for the second time that week he had chosen to override her 'irrational' fears of a haunting at Bramley Lodge. She was not irrational: the screams, the noises, the spectral woman, they were not figments of her own imagination, as he suggested. Nor were they 'cries for attention, from a bored, lonely housewife,' more scathing remarks she had had to endure, from the mouth of her beloved.

She had been frightened of this, that was why she had chosen to stay quiet, to fight her demons; those in her mind and those who stalked the halls of her home. She had feared that he would react in this horrid way, but why? She had been worried about his often-cold nature, the late evenings at work, the flicker of an affair with 'Caroline' that would not rest in her mind. Was it possible that she was afraid of him too? After all, he had suffered through some of the inexplicable, late night disturbances with her. What had made him so angry about his wife confessing her fears to him? Was it protection, of his house, his inheritance? James had lived in this house for years prior to meeting and marrying her. He had inherited it from his family; a long line of Steads had paced these floorboards, as she did now. But had they lived through the terror that she was experiencing? Had they been in fear of a strange woman who screamed her presence and shook the house to its very foundations? Had James never, sincerely, experienced an inkling of the strange happenings that she had encountered, over the last few months? She had so many questions and nothing but an icy trail of cold, frozen air left in James' wake to answer them.

She walked towards the front door, the air blowing from outside chilled her exposed face, even though the door had swung closed behind James' fury. Frost had gathered in the corners of each window pane; flecks of sleet streaked across the glass like teeth, carving out patterns. She reached for her overcoat, tempted with the pull of her usual morning walk, despite the freezing temperatures. She thought she might keep walking; maybe she would rid herself of the problem by ridding herself of all thoughts of James and his haunted, uncomfortable home. She stopped, startled, as a circular pattern began to unravel before her very eyes, on the glass of the front door. Misty circles unfurled, cracked and wispy, intricate; one form curling into another, enlarging the circle and then, all at once, fading, evaporating, disappearing from view, as if someone was breathing on the glass. Her blood ran cold as she imagined staring into the eyes of an unseen intruder; the same intruder whose deathly screams she had hidden from for all these months.

* * *

She shook the sparkling droplets from her overcoat and placed it back on the coat stand in the porch. She walked out of her boots, ruffling her skirt and wiping stray hairs from her face as she moved towards the warmth of the house. Her morning walk had been fuelled with anger; her strides long and desperate, crunching on the drifts of soft ice that had formed overnight, crushing the long grass shoots as she had walked, lost in her thoughts. She had almost forgotten about the breath on the glass pane that morning, the spectral tendrils of cold air that had, again, marked an unknown presence in the house.

Still, at the forefront of her mind, resided James and their earlier argument, his indifference to her fears and his anger towards her. With little way of reaching him throughout the day, she decided that it would waste time to consider the reasons behind his temper. He had been unreasonable and although he was perhaps tired from his work, maybe he was afraid too. Or perhaps his anger hid a much darker level of deception, a third person that he had allowed to creep into their marriage, almost unnoticed, her name whispered only as he slept.

She made her way to the kitchen. The maids had not worked that morning; it seemed unnecessary to keep them on a regular basis when May was at home day in, day out. There was hardly anything to do, or anyone to cook for, though May would be glad of the company.

On her way, she noticed the dark, cracked door of the cellar again; a room that stayed almost hidden from view, lost in the walled panels of the hallway, unless you were looking. She had not been looking for it, but today it was as if the door itself reached out to her, like a living, breathing being creaking to life. She stood still and heard nothing but the sound of her own deep breaths. She took in the lines of the wooden door, the tiny holes that peppered the top, the panels cracked and aged and the bolt flecked orange and rusty. This cellar had not been touched for years.

She thought, for a second, then found herself walking over, her feet arched almost in tiptoe, as if not to disturb anyone, living or dead. She reached her hand out to the panels, smoothing her fingers over the knots and splits. It was cold, solid; the guardian of the unknown, to her. She felt along the door for the bolt, the light dim in this corner of the house. Her fingers curled as she found the cold metal, almost freezing to the touch. Her mind was elsewhere, but her fingers wiggled the bolt, just to test it; a sharp screech of twisting metal and the bolt was slowly freeing itself from its clamp. How unexpected, she thought, both exhilarated and terrified.

She twisted the bolt several times, ignoring the ache in her fingers as she did; she eased the bolt free, the screeching drilling into her skull as she did. She almost jumped back in shock, when the door swung back, almost knocking her to the floor; its hinges squeaking, free from its restraints. A puff of dust clouded over her as the door swung back and forth on its hinges. Perhaps these fears of the unknown were over and she was now free to venture forth and find whatever her mind would allow.

In an effort to overcome her fear of the deep black of the cellar, she reached for an oil lamp that had been sat by the unseen door, discarded, for as long as she had lived there and, taking one careful step at a time, she let the darkness of the cellar doorway envelope her as she felt her way along a damp handrail. One by one, she descended the steps. The wood of the handrail felt clammy in her hands; she could not tell if it was the aged wood itself, or the sweat seeping from her fingertips. She was shaking, having to take deep breaths to steady her on the descent.

The light from the oil lamp was dim, but necessary, though the eerie shadows it cast along the walls made her heart flutter, shocked by the sudden movement of her own gigantic shadow, the fingers and legs extended into an unrecognisable, spindly creature. In the half-light, she could make out the remains of wallpaper scraps that looked to have been almost entirely scratched off the walls.

When she reached the bottom of the steps, she shone the lamplight around the room. It was smaller than she had imagined; having expected a sprawling room, with a low-beamed ceiling, spanning the length of the house itself. This cellar was no more than a large box shape, she found, as she edged around the room, the lamp held firm in front of her, darting the circular beam into each corner, each nook and cranny.

She walked to the far wall, just a few metres from where she had stood at the bottom of the steps. Placing her hands on the cold wall, it felt solid to the touch, although a mass of what looked to be dark grey, damp patches had set in along the bottom of the wall. Could it be a draught, she wondered?

Something compelled her to look further, without wanting to make any noise, for fear of waking the entities of Bramley. She curled her left hand into a fist and rapped, timid and unsure, on the wall. An echo. A slight, almost incoherent echo of her knocking, bounced back from the wall. The texture felt softer, an inexplicable difference to the solid walls that she had felt her way around. It did not move, yet its foundations felt somewhat unsteady.

She knocked again; this time louder, her fist braver, stronger than the last. The echo bounced back again, stronger, in tune with hers. She knocked a third time, louder again, the echo returned her call. What could be causing the echo? She thought, rapping again, waiting for the immediate echo. Could this be a false wall? Suddenly, something else emitted from behind the partition; something darker, something familiar. Beyond the wall that separated her from whatever lay beyond it came that all too familiar scream, the guttural screech of a pained beast. And she wasted no time in fleeing the confines of the cellar, where her deepest fears of that unknown room, that had lain so insignificant and hidden, had been confirmed.

She gasped as she felt the warmth of the upstairs rooms, the hint of frosted daylight clawing at her face as she ascended the final two steps away from the cellar. She caught her breath and slammed the door shut, wrenching the bolt across as she did so, before sinking to her knees in exhaustion. It had all led to this: the noises; the strange screaming figure that roamed the halls of her home, the argument with James. She had given in to the pull of the cellar and its secrets and, though it had given her no answers, she was frightened and confused; left to wonder if there was another space, hidden behind the deceit of the grey matter that her fingers had explored.

She would have to go back. But not today. There was too much whirring around in her mind: images of James' angry retreat, the woman with the gaping mouth and the strange, unsteady feeling of the wall, played through her mind, winding tighter and tighter until, feeling a wave of hideous nausea, she placed her head in her hands.

A fleeting movement brought her back to her senses. The house dropped to a freezing temperature. To the left, a flash of white, all too familiar, moving between rooms. She was not alone, again. She released her head from her hands as she dared to raise her eyes to the end of the hall. Her breath stopped short as she caught sight of the screaming woman. She was frozen to the spot by an icy breeze emitting from the entity, whose face was twisted in a silent scream, a dark hole in the middle of her face from which the breeze emanated.

She could not take her eyes from the woman, who stood, motionless but threatening, her only movements in her face, twisted in pain or desperation. Did she know that she could not be heard? Her deep black, inky hair still cascaded in wild curls around her head, her dress appeared torn at the edges and flowing around her unseen feet, as if she were levitating. The figure moved, propelled forward. May attempted to stand, her legs scrabbled under her, failing her as they shook in the presence of woman.

The screaming figure's movements were slow, distorted, as she floated above the ground; the wooden floorboards visible beneath her. She made no distinct footsteps, much like the shadowy figure that had haunted May's dreams. The angel that had stopped at each door along the top hallway had, in fact, bore the twisted face of a ravaged demon, a tormented soul that sought not to help, perhaps even to kill.

She lifted her face to see the woman once more. With renewed strength, she found her voice and, before she could comprehend what she was doing, she spoke to the entity that drifted closer to her, as if mocking her fear.

'WHO ARE YOU?' She questioned the spirit, in clear, sharp control.

The figure said nothing, her mouth still contorted in a silent scream, her arms flailing at the sides as she edged closer still. She was centimetres away from her, now, the wisps of her torn dress licking at the floor like serpents; a blast of cold air and she was towering above her. A face that had held many nightmares, that softened as she bent down, to taunt further. A face that pressed into hers, a feeling of a thousand ice-picks hacking at her skin, as if the figure itself was raking at her face, clawing to get in. And somewhere, in the depths of her mind, the figure spoke one word; the last word she heard before everything turned black.

'Caroline.'

* * *

December 18th, 1885

My Dearest Sister-In-Law,

It is with deepest sympathy that I must write to you, regarding your sister, my wife, May.

I cannot begin to express my sadness, as I must tell you that she is missing, though we are not at liberty to make presumptions as to where she may be at this time.

By now, you will have been made aware by your Mother that May was not herself in the last few days before her disappearance. She had been suffering hallucinations of the most terrifying kind that may have triggered her desire to leave me and to leave Bramley Lodge. She spoke of irrational fears that she was being haunted by the ghost of a screaming spirit; a woman who she claimed stalked the grounds of Bramley. Whilst I have no reason to believe these sightings to have been anything more than tricks of the mind, I only wish I had realised her psychosis sooner, so that I might have been able to treat her here, in the safety of our home.

It has been two days since May's disappearance, two agonising days that have left me baffled and increasingly worried for her safety. I have notified the police and they are combing the countryside for signs of her whereabouts. Neighbouring villages have been informed to be on the lookout.

I send my sincere apologies. As I write to you with such worrying news, I can only beg that, should you hear anything from her, please urge her to contact me, her husband, so we might be able to reconcile and that I might be able to help her and bring her home, to where she rightfully belongs.

Yours, forever faithfully

Dr James Stead

* * *

She did not know for how long she had been unconscious. Lifting her head from the cold, hard stone, each bone in her body ached and her fingers felt as though they were on fire. Even the skin on her eyelids burned; her eyelashes had clumped together with moisture that had long since dried. It could have been hours or days, all sense of time was lost.

She bent her legs and crawled slowly to a crouching position, her ankles taking the weight of her as she dragged her arms to support the weight of her tired body. It was as if she was waking from a dream, Memories rushed, blurring into each other, strangers, colours, experiences, all misplaced and jumbled, adding to the stabbing pain in her head. She blinked again. She wiped a layer of dust, or grime from her face and attempted to open her eyes again, to focus on the space that she was in.

It was as if she was plunged into darkness again; not a dreamlike darkness, but tangible and thick, as if the unknown space had swallowed her.

A faint memory sparked in her aching, confused mind. A woman -not a woman, but an entity - gliding towards her. She gasped to herself as she remembered the last possible stream of consciousness that she could lay claim to. She remembered her fear; the unknown, the impossible confrontation with the being that had invaded her life. Her movements became more erratic; she remembered the way that the being moved, the way she taunted her, her face gaping in that hideous, constant scream. She felt along the floor, hopeful for something: a light, a sign, a clue as to where she was. Her fingers were shaking with nerves as she felt her fear of the woman rising again, like bile, an uncontrollable sickness. Her fingers searched, scrabbling along the floor, until they hit against something solid. She picked it up with both hands, feeling along the object in her temporary, uneasy blindness, guessing what was in front of her. She was momentarily taken back to her childhood; party games with her sister flashed before her, blind man's buff, the childish way that she would spin around, blindfolded, without a care in the world. Where was her sister? Would she be worried?

The object was wide and rectangular in shape; it felt cold to the touch, like metal. She felt along its sides until she found a handle, then felt her way down along a grate of wire – a lamp! A lamp! She guided her hands back to the blackness, to find matches, oil, anything that would light the lamp, that would light her way out of the dark, back to the house, back to James. Oh James! He must be worried sick.

It took a few moments to find some matches, discarded on the floor. She presumed that they had been left there in a hurry, by someone. Though her hands were still shaking, she struck the match and held it to the lamp, turning her face away as the brightness shocked her, the heat burning into her face. She allowed her eyes to adjust to the dim light of the room, before turning back; the full flare stinging her face, her skin crawling under the glare of its warmth. Raising the lamp, she took in the room around her, plain yet familiar. Three dark walls surrounded her, with stripped remnants of wallpaper. She was facing a set of steps leading up to an old, wooden panelled door. The floor was a deep concrete with nothing more than little scratches and etches that had worn into it over time. Her fingers dug into the etches. She was in the cellar.

She placed the lamp behind her and cautiously swung her feet around, wincing in pain. It was only then, in the dim but sufficient light of the lamp, that she noticed how dirty she was. Her dress was covered in a film of bright, settled dust, iridescent in the lamplight. She glanced around, satisfied that there was nobody in the cellar with her, before she turned to face the fourth wall. She remembered the knocking; the strange echoes, the conclusion that the wall, may indeed, have been false. And with that, she lifted the lamp from the floor again, and fell back in horror.

Across the fourth wall, were hundreds of holes; large holes, as if the wall had been scratched, hammered and torn through. There were cracks in places, where the wall had been pulled apart. She glanced around, to scour the floor again, but could see no tools that would have aided such work. She steadied herself for a few minutes, taking in the strangeness, then stretched to her feet to inspect the broken wall.

As she stepped closer, the pain pounded in her bones. Her hands felt excruciating, but she felt no draught blowing towards her, as she had felt before. No breeze flickered through the torn holes or cracks that littered the wall and, as she edged closer still, she could see no daylight, no sign of outside, of life. Her suspicions had been right; this wall was rectified to protect whatever lay behind it and, though she had no answers, she was compelled to venture further.

She squinted, willing her eyes to see shapes and shadows that danced in the blackness, beyond the wall. The lamp was dimming; she shuddered at the thought of being plunged into darkness again. She placed her hands along the largest gap in the wall and winced as loose grains from the disturbed wall knocked against her fingers, now bloody and cut. She stared further into the hole, lifting the light to see the blank space.

An object.

The slow swing of the lamp caught the silhouette of a shape, placed in the middle of the floor. The room had looked almost as big as the room she was in; bare, apart from the shape: square, almost oblong, though she had no time to decipher it. She swung the light again, a second, third and fourth time; catching glimpses of the box's shape but the light would not stay still for long enough to illuminate any detail.

She shifted her hands in the hole, pushing further forwards, to make a bigger hole. Everything from her elbows was swallowed by the darkness; she was unable to see any movement in front of her. The lamp dimmed again, she was running out of time. She pushed against the wall again, ducking under crumbling sounds coming from all around her. She pushed at the loosening hole and widened it further, enough to provide more movement for her hands and for the swinging lamp. Pushing the light further through the gap, again, she gasped as it illuminated the strange shadow placed, as if on purpose, in the centre of the floor. A black box, a miniature museum, that contained nothing, but the remains of a human skull.

She dropped the light and fear rushed through what little she could still feel of her body in the freezing cellar. She bent down to seek out the lamp again. The outline of that macabre, trapped shape, the skull, whirred through her mind as a familiar sound rose from the depths of the house. A scream, *the* scream, the terrified voice of someone, or something trapped in an unseen world, only feet away from her. She scrambled to her feet, her body jolted into action, by the blood curdling sound and the shrouded memories of the terror she had felt, in this house, since she had married James and moved to Bramley Lodge.

***

James. Would he know where to find her? How long had she been here? Why had he not come to her? These thoughts raced through her mind, sweeping her along with them, as she resolved that she must try to find a way out; a way back. Forgetting the dying oil lamp, she felt along the walls for support and made her way across the small space of the cellar, to the familiar footfalls of the staircase. Each movement was slow and deliberate. The pitch black of the cellar swept across her, again, as the oil lamp gave out the last of its light.

A light, swift and sudden, burned into her retinas as it swept across the vast room. Each step unfurled in the warm light; a consuming light she had not seen for so long. A shadow stood at the top of the stairs, stooping, she could make out no features, only the foreboding sense of a man. James. She blinked upwards and reached for him as he descended the staircase to meet her. He had found her, though his descent was slow, deliberate; she could make out no facial features as the light from upstairs glared behind him, his bulking shadow stretching across the walls as he stepped closer. She ignored the fear, the bile as it rose from her stomach, silently reassuring herself that it was over and yet, the skull, the screams, the sense of fear that her husband had evoked, caused her to shiver with fear.

James' face looked contorted, demonic, as he drew near to her. He reached a hand to stop her shaking bones, but she ignored the feeling of crawling skin, he did not pacify her. For a moment, his eyes shone with familiarity; she was transported to her wedding day, to the first time she had met him, his handsome features beaming at her, his eyes full of promise, of lust. And then she saw his smile twist. He was no longer the man she believed she had loved; he was as much a demon as the ghost who had terrorised her these seasons past. He pointed towards the broken wall; the terrible truth behind it became all too clear and hideous for her. His words came rushing forth with a gust of freezing wind,

"I see you've met Caroline," as he gestured towards the concealed skull hidden behind the wall. "You should have left well alone May; you should have left alone."

And she realised then, that the phantoms of her nightmares had, indeed, taken on a very real and terrifying face; the face of the man, the monster she had married.

And as the last blow fell upon her, bludgeoning her exquisite face, she thought only of her sister and of her mother and of that faraway townhouse that had kept her safe for so long, from monsters, both living and dead and the men that will kill to conceal them.

* * *

9th January, 1883

My Dearest Sister-In-Law Anne,

It has now been three weeks since I last knew the whereabouts of my beloved Caroline. I have lived in hope that she will return to me; that we will continue to live at Bramley, as loving husband and wife and that you will find it in your heart to forgive me for losing such a precious and beautiful woman. But it is all, I fear, to no avail.

Caroline was last seen wandering the grounds of Bramley three weeks ago. I imagine she would have been wearing her long black overcoat and the wonderful hat with the peacock feather, that I had bought her as a wedding gift. It was her most favourite item of clothing. Whilst I know it will be of little comfort to you in these troubling and tragic times, I must insist that Caroline seemed to be in a most happy of moods, just before her sudden absence. However, I feel I must admit to you that she had also been suffering from incomprehensible night terrors. She talked often of a most horrid nightmare that had plagued her, here at Bramley; a ghost of a lost woman who would wander the halls and terrorise her in her sleep. I fear, dear Anne, that your sister was not well at all and that I, as her dutiful husband, had overlooked the psychological impact that such terrors may have caused her.

But, alas, three weeks on and I cannot keep my hopes held high for her safe return. I fear I have truly lost Caroline forever and, in doing so, I must also write with my most sincere of apologies for your loss; for all that I may have caused through my ignorance and misunderstanding of Caroline's wellbeing. You must rest assured that the authorities have been informed and that we will continue our search for Caroline, though I remain unsure that you or I will see her again. Please know that I will keep her close to my heart, close to me, and that I will love her forever more.

Yours Most Saddened,

Dr James Stead.

MOVING ON

The sound of gravel as it chipped against the tyres of my car was almost overpowering, as I reversed away from the drive for the last time, like miniature bullets as they struck against the body work. I had always hated that sound, revered by his decision to remove the wildly overgrown front garden patches and make way for metre upon metre of white stone. It had always felt clinical, somehow. Much like the gravel chipping away at my car, it had been those overriding decisions that had chipped away at our marriage over the next ten years. What had been a dispute about the mess of our new front garden had become bickering and arguing over almost every room in the house. Isn't it funny how something so small, so every day, can stir up such emotion? But still, I reversed, with the remnants of past arguments echoing in my head, as I hit the brake and drove away, without so much as a backward glance.

The truth was, I was less than enamoured with the idea of staying at my parents' house over the next few months, just until I found a place of my own. I was lucky to be in the market to buy my own place and, whilst I knew the area I wanted to live in (as far away from him as possible), I knew I needed to give myself time to settle, time to heal from a ten-year rift.

Ted and I had agreed to sell the cottage and both move out to other, newer properties. Financially I suppose it made sense, but there was something about the place, the past that it had housed, that left me almost breathless in those first few months of awkward separation. I had always believed that the walls of buildings could be scarred by what they witnessed, by what they housed. There was something that breathed in the walls of the cottage, that would forever replay memories that I would rather forget. I had made the discovery amount 6 months ago, the usual tell-tale signs that the mind wants you not to see; the late-night phone calls and the garbled excuses for late finishes at work, it all made sense to me. I had not cried from that moment, I felt a sense of relief wash over me as I had heard the satisfying click of disconnection and replaced my phone on the hook. Done. Disconnected. Over.

I was told by most that I should be thankful there were few complications with the separation - I mean, thank Christ we didn't have children. He wanted to, but then he wanted everything his older brothers had. I always had to fight against his advances and his overbearing nature. The timing never felt right. Nor the person, if I am honest. Which I can be, because I drove away from that place with not another thought or care about him or us. And though I never voiced my annoyance at their breezy opinions, I somewhat disagreed that there were no complications. Aside from the sale of the house, there would always be complications in matters of the heart.

My first night at my parent's home was comfortable, though I had to sleep in the confines of my old bedroom, which appeared to house some sort of shrine to my teenage years. I had been joyously plied with my favourite wine and a takeaway, supplied by my lovely parents upon my arrival, hoping to ease the pain of my move and my failed marriage, before I shipped myself off to bed, leaving half of my luggage in the hallway. I was too tired to start rooting through more memories. Half of the room had been redecorated in an attempt to make it beige, more 'guest-room' worthy, yet half of the walls were still dotted with faded certificates and old posters, their corners hanging away from my mother's attempts to re-stick them. There were polaroid photos, snaps of days out with old friends that had been precariously jammed into the sides of the mirror that hung opposite my bed. I had sighed a wistful sigh as I put my light out that night, not longing for those days, but longing for the innocence of them.

That first night, I fell into a deep sleep that was almost dreamless, though shapes and figures sprang into my slumbering mind as soon as my head hit the pillow. I had always assumed that the faceless shapes in my dreams of late had been my subconscious trying to make sense of the woman my husband had had an affair with. My mind had reached out for more answers or comparisons, whilst my logical brain wanted nothing to do with her, despite my natural curiosity.

In this dream, however, I saw the figure of a lady, an older woman who moved close to my mind's eye as I asked her name. She looked older, though her features were blackened in the kind of dreamscape you often find yourself seeing things through blurred lenses, as if she was emerging from a tunnel. A shadow at first, though I don't remember feeling afraid, she held both hands out to me, as if welcoming me towards her.

The persistent ring of the telephone on the upstairs landing woke me up, its shrill pitch bore into my brain, which felt somewhat dizzy from the wine I had consumed. I sat up and looked at the clock, my eyes adjusted to the black metal hands as they wound around a harsh clock face, it was already 9 a.m. With the sound of the phone still ringing through me, I reached for my dressing gown, which was slung over the chair at the end of the bed, and scrabbled out of bed to answer.

"Hello?" My tone was tentative, I was conscious of answering a phone in a house I wasn't supposed to be living in.

"Hello," the voice replied, I relaxed at the recognition of Julia Fairfax's soft tone, my estate agent. "Can I speak to Mrs Walters please?"

"Speaking," I managed a half-smile, though I still felt groggy from the rude awakening.

"Ah," Julia replied, "Amanda, how are you? Settling in well at your mum's?"

"Well," I looked around me for signs of life, assuming both my parents had vacated for work that day. "Sort of. It's strange to be here again, full time."

"Well," Julia's voice sounded hopeful. "It might not be for long, I have a house that has come on the market this morning AND it's in the area you were specifically looking at."

"Really?" I needed to sit down, I was not expecting something to come up so soon. "Tell me more."

So, Amanda told me about the house, whilst speaking in excited tones as she described its cottage-style interior and brick exterior. It sounded small, but perfectly formed for one with one large bedroom and a guest bedroom in the attic and a comfortably-sized living area. And no gravel. I had taught myself to be dubious of her over-excitement, convinced that she could show too much enthusiasm for a shoe box if it would lead to a sale, but then again, her heart was in the right place.

I was reluctant to organise a showing straightaway, the tiredness I was feeling was pounding through my head, as the events of the last few days had caught up with me. Part of me wanted to drag myself back under the covers for a few hours, desperate to catch up on sleep and allow myself to wallow in my uncertainty for a little longer. But there was a pull too, something inexplicable, that tugged and whispered of missed opportunities and freedom. And it was that tiny, almost insignificant pull that brought me to the front of an unfamiliar house later that afternoon.

***

Julia was running late, or so I presumed, as I checked the clock on my phone once more, hoping for a missed call or a message from her. But there was nothing, a blank space and no explanation. I looked up at the house, aware that my car had been parked at the end of the driveway for over half an hour and anxious about the twitching curtains of concerned, nearby residents, I debated whether to take a walk up to the house and get a feel for the place from the outside. At least I would be doing something, other than sitting and fretting, and the curtains may cease to twitch for a while. I threw my phone back into the depths of my bag and reached for the door handle.

A light drizzle of rain had started to mist around the car as I locked it behind me, feeling myself almost tiptoeing as I walked up towards the house, careful of my intrusion on another person's space. It looked empty from a distance, there were no signs of any movement, the shadowy shuffling of everyday life going on behind closed doors, no flicker of lights as occupants moved between rooms. The house was not mine and yet, as I got nearer to it, taking in the details in front of me, that had been nothing more than adjectives and selling words from Julia on the phone earlier that day, it almost started to take on a different shape. The unfamiliarity began to melt away as my mind flickered with images of another me, older and happier and settled, but here. I shook my head at such a strange notion, though I felt uncomfortable at how comfortable I was beginning to feel.

The house had been on the market for several months, according to my earlier phone conversation with Julia, though I struggled to see why. Apart from its more remote location, which was appealing to me, the house appeared to be perfect for professionals or even a young family, looking to live in a more rural environment. I hadn't asked about the previous occupants, not wishing to form an opinion too early on, and only too aware of how much a house can live and breathe its history from the place I had left behind. A fresh start for me meant viewing a new living space as a blank canvas, imagining myself moving pieces of my life, my habits, my rituals into new walls and spaces, I did not want to feel myself stepping into someone else's shoes.

In many ways, the house looked to be a similar layout to the house I had previously lived in; a renovated cottage with a modern feel, though this place looked a tad more dated. The brickwork was patchy in places, and sparse growths of wildflowers ran along the front fascia, stopping at a central wooden front door, which had once been a deep crimson colour, but was now faded and peeling along the wooden panels. The windows were in much the same condition, the once-white wooden panels were now faded and dirtied to a washed grey colour, their hinges now splayed bright orange with rust. The old house had a perfect box of clean lines and perpendicular bricks, this place looked rough around the edges, cracked in places and yet somehow, it already felt like home. My eyes followed the cracks in the front wall as it twisted up towards the gaping windows of the upper floors and I almost jumped as I noticed the figure in the top window, returning my gaze.

***

Startled, I was back at the front gate, trying to get hold of Julia again, since I had heard nothing from her in the past half an hour. I had frantically backed off after meeting the gaze of the shrouded figure in the window, certain that nobody would be in the house, I felt like I had trespassed, my presence unexpected, as unexpected as the person in the window. I looked at the clock on my phone again, it was fast approaching 2 p.m. and still I had heard no word from Julia, the reception bar on my phone was blurring between one and two bars, despite holding it up above my head, like a strange antenna.

I glanced back at the house, unnerved but unsure why I was, there had been no reason to assume the house was not currently lived in. The front door stood ajar, its crimson paint stood in shadow at its new angle. It was as if the house and its unexpected occupant were acknowledging me and inviting me in, though I could no longer see anyone in view. I was taken aback by this – knowing that I had been spotted but the lack of direct communication concerned me, with no definite word from Julia I was torn between driving home and rescheduling a viewing when it was more convenient for Julia and walking back up to the house with hopes of a sneaky look around whilst the owner was still there. After some deliberation and cowering against the droplets of rain as they bulged from an ever-greying sky, I resolved that the owner was probably used to visitors, especially with the length of time that the house had been on the market. They were perhaps not precious about allowing strangers in to look around - and that I was no cause for concern anyway, just nosey at best. I stalked my way back up towards the house, taking in the eerie but comfortable quiet around me as I approached the half open door.

I knocked on the small brass door knocker twice, the first was tentative, the second harder as I was now competing against a heavier breeze. I still felt myself jump as the door was pulled back to reveal a small woman; an older lady of about sixty-five, or thereabouts, with a look of surprise on her face. She was much shorter than I was, though she walked with a very slight hunchback which made her appear shorter, still. Her hair was white with wild curls that were thinning at the ends and she was wearing a faded summer dress with a blue polka-dot pattern and a thin woollen shawl just covering her shoulders. Her face was open and friendly, though she looked confused. She had the kind of eyes that smiled, they were the deep grey colour of the clouds above us, shrouded by fine lines and a dusting of a half-applied blue eyeshadow that matched her dress.

"I'm so sorry to interrupt," I began, not wishing to worry the lady. "I had a viewing booked today with Julia, only she hasn't arrived."

"Oh," the woman replied, slowly but with force. "You haven't heard then."

"No," I replied. "I don't seem to have any reception on my phone out here, I've tried calling her but I suppose she's been held up."

"Don't worry dear," a smile grew across her face as she continued to speak. "I was told to expect you. Please come in, you're more than welcome to come and look around."

"Honestly I don't wish to intrude Mrs…" I stopped as I realised I had no idea what the lady's name was.

"Price, dear," she filled in the gap. "Mrs Price. I would be happy to show you around, like I said, I was told you would be coming."

And with that, she held the door open and ushered me into the house. I could not have been more grateful at that moment to be stepping into a dry house, as the first clap of thunder rolled somewhere in the distance.

Once we were inside, the place had an instant warmth about it. The hallway was barely decorated with a line of small shoes placed against one wall and a selection of coat hooks on the other. The ceilings felt low as I entered, as if I was in a cottage, but the hallway led into a spacious kitchen and living room area, which was every bit as perfectly jumbled as the photographs had suggested on the website. The furniture was mismatched, each piece was worn and beautiful, surrounded by stacks of magazines and books, of photographs, as if pieces of a well-lived life were all stuffed in to every nook and cranny. Compared to the minimalism that had been imposed on me in my last house, my previous life, it was almost cluttered. But it didn't deter me from imagining where I would place my own furniture, my own trinkets and memories, placing myself and my own life into the corners of this secluded little home.

Mrs Price had disappeared around the corner, into the kitchen area. I followed through to the kitchen, calling after her having heard some sort of cluttering noise echoing through. I was surprised to find nobody there, though two mugs were placed along the worktop as if she had been about to serve tea. A tap dripped into the sink, almost in time with the light rain that was now hitting against the window panes. There was a deathly quiet about the place I felt, as I stood motionless listening to the dripping water, powerful above the silence.

"Tea?" Mrs Price called to me, I spun around to face her, stunned by her sudden shrill voice.

"Oh," I replied, smoothing my dress down as I settled. "Yes please."

"Kettle has not long boiled," Mrs Price's face creased into another friendly smile. "Sugar?"

"One, please," I replied, taking a seat at the small wooden table, watching Mrs Price as she busied herself around the kitchen. She seemed tranquil, almost in her own world as I suppose elderly people who are accustomed to living alone do. I laughed a little to myself as I imagined this to be me in several years, my marriage had left me craving nothing but solitude in my relatively young age, the peace and quiet that I had experienced in this house had been warming, comforting in such discomforting times, it had begun to feel like my home. I came back to my senses and glanced up at Mrs Price as she strained the teabags, but it was as if she was staring through me.

Time itself seemed to stand still as we sat at Mrs Price's kitchen table and talked about the house that she had lived in for over thirty-five years. She talked little about her husband, now deceased, though she did speak fondly of her two children, both now grown and living away. I sat and listened as she talked of the very things in her life that created the fabric of her home; birthday parties and long summers spent making dens in the garden, the first visits from baby grandchildren, the first day she moved in with her young husband, vibrant and ready for life as a married couple and the last day he left.

"So, you obviously love the house, Mrs Price," I questioned. "Why is it that you wish to sell it now?"

"That's a good question, my dear," Mrs Price replied, placing her mug on the table. "I suppose I think it's time for me, to move on. Everything has its place, dear, it's someone else's turn now, to make new memories in this place."

As she spoke, she raised her eyes to look around, as if haunted by the memories that tumbled from her. I was a near enough stranger and yet she openly told me stories about her life, as if she was enticing me in to pick up where she would leave. We planned to finish our drinks and then take a tour of the upstairs bedrooms and the garden, if the rain would allow, though the droplets seemed heavier as they smashed against the kitchen window.

"I think you would be perfect for a place like this," Mrs Price had said when I queried how many other potential buyers had booked viewings. I had thought it strange at the time that she didn't comment on the place being perfect for me, it was as if she was testing me as a worthy buyer of her home. I could hardly complain though, I had heard horror stories about house sales falling through because occupants couldn't bear to part with the houses, hostile owners who would do everything in their power to put potential buyers off purchasing a property. Mrs Price had a personality that warmed the very house itself; it was perhaps intimidating to have the honour of filling such well-loved shoes in a place that has breathed so much joy into Mrs Price's life, for so long. We both swigged the dregs of our tea which were now lukewarm at the bottom of their china cups.

I glanced at the clock in the kitchen, distracted by the loud ticking noise that emanated from it, whilst Mrs Price gathered the teacups and made herself busy in the kitchen again, promising a slice of cake that she was sure she had wrapped up in a cupboard, somewhere. Somewhere in the distance, I heard a siren whizz past, the first noise from a road that I had noticed since entering the house. That was when I noticed that there were no hands on the clock, even though its persistent ticking was loud and clear. The numbers were still etched in a classic italic font around the edge of the round clock face, but it was skewed and bare, with the absence of ticking hands. I racked my brains trying to remember if I had noticed such a thing when I first entered. But my mind was clouded with the views of the house that I had taken in, with Mrs Price's endless tales, I could not remember seeing or indeed not seeing the hands on the clock face.

"Do you want another?" Mrs Price's muffled voice called out from inside a cupboard. "I'll put the kettle on if you do."

Before I could answer, a knock at the door stopped Mrs Price in her search, she poked her head around the door, excusing herself to answer, I waved my hands as if to reassure her that she should think nothing of it. After all, I was the stranger here. Not being able to fully explain the clock on the wall, I put it down to being an old piece of furniture that Mrs Price kept for sentimental purposes, rather than for function. Still, the ticking persisted, timeless. I heard Mrs Price talking at the front door, though the voices were hushed and I could make out nothing of the conversation. I resolved to help Mrs Price by refilling the kettle.

My glasses steamed up as I poured the residue water from the kettle, feeling strangely comfortable with finding my way around the kitchen. I turned the tap to full, to release the water into the kettle, but felt my body jolt as a noise crashed above me. It sounded as if something had fallen over, a huge or heavy object that had slipped out of careless hands. I stopped for a second, but thought nothing more of it as I continued to fill the kettle, listening to the muffled sounds of Mrs Price's conversation by the front door. What happened next was harder to ignore, as I placed the kettle back on its stand and fumbled for the power switch, I was disturbed by the distinct sound of footsteps running overhead. Mrs Price lived here alone, from what she had said there was nobody else staying with her. The noise was clear, each step was quick and deliberate as it paced above me, racing along the top floor, dissipating as it ran away. I jumped as it happened a second time and a third; it was the sound of an excited child or someone running late. There was no other sound, no voice as the unknown person collided with Mrs Price, it seemed to run and stop, never descending the stairs or reaching its destination.

"My dear," Mrs Price appeared back in the kitchen again, her face somewhat ashen, though still smiling. "Sorry about that."

"Do you have someone staying with you, Mrs Price?" I asked bluntly, unnerved by the footsteps that had echoed above me.

"No, dear," she replied, "I already told you, I live alone."

"I heard footsteps," I said, raising my eyes to where I had heard them. "As if someone was running above my head."

"Strange," she said, almost shrugging off my claim. "There is nobody here but me."

The rumbling sound of the boiling kettle brought me back to the present, I explained that I thought I would put the kettle on, whilst Mrs Price was answering the door, but could sense that her tone had slightly changed. She was still friendly and warm, to an extent, but she seemed almost wary of me. Mrs Price joined me at the worktop and took over the tea making, she was in no hurry to show me out and I hadn't ventured upstairs yet, though I felt reluctant to, with the sound of footsteps still echoing in my head.

I became conscious of the time, with no feasible way of reading it in the house, I remembered I had placed my handbag in the hallway when I first entered. I excused myself to check the time and for any messages from Julia, it seemed to have grown darker since I had entered the house, though the increasing rain and grey clouds would not have helped, the house itself still felt bright and airy, plenty of natural light pouring through the windows. And yet, I felt uneasy in the house, with the sound of ghost footsteps and Mrs Price's subtle but strange change in behaviour. My handbag was still slumped in the hallway; the contents of it were spilling a little over, where I had left it unzipped. I reached inside for my phone, fumbling until I could feel the familiar cold metal of my mobile. I turned the phone over and felt for the switch and watching the screen illuminate before me, I was confused as the digits blinked at me.

1:57

The last time I had looked at my phone, it had read the same time. It had been approaching 2p.m. when I had exited my car, losing hope of Julia's appearance at our scheduled meeting. I turned the phone over in my hands, attempting to switch the screen on but it was frozen. The battery symbol still appeared full and I had had no problems with the life of the phone itself, but I felt nothing but frustration at its timely decision to freeze. Judging by the amount of time I felt I had been in the house, I judged that at least one hour had passed and, feeling disorientated without any knowledge of the actual time, I resolved to cut my stay short and head home. I threw my phone back in my bag, annoyed at its uselessness and walked back through to Mrs Price, as the sound of another distant siren echoed somewhere along the road.

"I hadn't realised the time," I said, not wishing to alarm Mrs Price. "I really should be going, you have been so kind to let me in though."

"No need to rush, dear," her response was alarming, though I supposed she was not used to visitors living as remote as she did. "Did you want to look upstairs?"

"Actually," I replied, feeling my tone sharpen in my resolve to get back home. "I think I'll try and ring Julia when I get home. Perhaps I could come back with her later in the week? Have a proper look around and talk more about the place?"

Mrs Price's eyes glazed over, they were a glassy blue but looked almost like ice as she sat in the chair, the heavy rainstorms now gathering pace and hitting around her at the window panes. She gave me a knowing smile, her silence disturbed something within me, though I could not work out what she was trying to say. I only knew that I wanted to leave the house, that the brightness and warmth that had struck me from the first viewing had changed somehow.

"Suit yourself," Mrs Price said, after a short time. "We have plenty of time."

And with that, I left my half-drunk teacup on the table and began to walk back towards the hallway, Mrs Price proffered me a hand as if offering to show me out. All at once I heard the footsteps again, this time, clattering above our heads as someone raced with urgency along the top floor, never completing their journey.

"Tell me you don't hear that, Mrs Price," my tone was soft but I meant what I said. All of a sudden, I felt as if she was hiding something, perhaps something that could affect the sale of the house. I wanted to know who had been at the door, who she had been talking to. Though I knew it was none of my business, that I had been a trespasser on her property all along.

"They don't bother me," Mrs Price smiled. "Memories, that's all."

"Well," I could feel breath getting shorter, alarmed by her calm nature towards the crashing above, snippets of old ghost stories and films I had seen over the years were playing in my mind, I needed to leave. "Thank you for your time, Julia will be in touch."

"I'm sure," Mrs Price's voice was slower as she spoke, as if she was running low on energy, she was making no sense and yet, I felt she was keeping something from me.

I grabbed my bag and fumbled for the cardigan I had slung up in the hallway when I had arrived, and saw myself out, not stopping to look back at Mrs Price as I flung the door open and made my way back down the driveway.

***

I had left my car parked at the end of the drive, not wishing to intrude on the space when I had arrived earlier. As I walked away from the house, unable to shake the feeling of dread in my stomach, I was met with an almost dreamlike scene. A distant blue light flashed atop a white car that was blocking the end of the driveway. As I moved closer I could see another car parked behind it, a generic dark green car with the passenger door wide open, as if someone had made a hurried exit.

An accident.

I was confused, remembering the distant sirens I had heard intermittently when I had been sat with Mrs Price, how had I not heard the commotion? I walked closer still, supposing that the knock at the door had been a police or ambulance official, supposing that Mrs Price had perhaps wanted to protect me from the scene by trying to persuade me from staying longer. And I thought nothing more of her strange behaviour until I moved closer still and saw the wrecked car that had been obscured by the cars around them

There were small groups of uniformed paramedics and policemen in clusters around the car. Someone sat in the driver's seat of the green car being consoled by a policeman, they looked up at me as I passed by, but did not react, they placed their head in their hands, tears streaming down their face. I approached two people, presumably police officers, who were taking notes and discussing the collision together,

"Parked up she was," I heard one of them say.

"Around the corner and out of nowhere," the other police officer replied.

"Excuse me," I tried to get their attention, for though I was less than a metre away from them, neither one had noticed me. "Can you please tell me what's happened?"

"When will they be moving the body?" The first officer spoke as if I hadn't said a word.

"Excuse me," I shouted again. "I was just visiting this house, I need to find my car. Can you please tell me what's happened?"

Still there was no reply from either officer. Without thinking, I stuck my arms in the air and waved them around, conscious that I must have looked like a lunatic but too afraid and confused to care. I shouted again for help, but not one of the nine or ten people who surrounded me answered, I could not be seen. And then it struck me, despite my concern at being ignored by the uniformed officials around me, I realised that although I could see the rain as it pounded against the ground, I could no longer feel it on my skin or clothing, the storms had gathered for most of the afternoon and yet, when I felt along my own arms I could feel nothing.

The feeling of dread returned as I turned to face the car that had remained obscured. I recognised it straight away as I walked towards it, taking in the scrape alongside the left-hand side of the car that had ruptured the metal, like some piece of giant machinery had torn the car open from one side. The side windows were smashed and the car had been thrown to one side, crushed into the side of a tree which now lay withered and draped over the terrible scene, as if in mourning.

I felt tears streaming down my face as I stared through the gaping window of the passenger seat at the silhouette of the body slumped in the driver's seat, obscured by the hanging trees that crushed against the car. Tears for what had happened, for the dead body or for what lingered on; because I knew without seeing the face beneath the gore. Because I knew that face well, it was mine.

***

I had always believed that the walls of buildings could be scarred by what they witnessed, by what they housed. There was something that breathed in the walls of the cottage, that would forever replay memories. Though I had no memory of what had been, whether my life had flashed before me in the last few moments or whether I had even felt the pain of being ripped from this world into the next. I had vague memories of exiting the car and the last thing I knew, I was being ushered inside by Mrs Price and the ghosts that lived within her walls.

She knew.

I was stood at the bottom of the driveway again, the rain misting around me though I felt nothing to touch, it was as if I had become invisible to the world and its elements, because I had. I could still feel my blood coursing through my body, my emotions ran high as I remembered my parents and how I wished I could have been near them again, as they were told the news. But I was confined to the spot, to this place, not because of what I had experienced, but because of what it had witnessed.

The door opened again, pushed back on its hinges and shining in the fading light of day, Mrs Price appeared, staring at me, not through me. She must have known when I arrived on her doorstep that I was not meant to be there. That I was keeping to a timetable that no longer existed. I began to take steps towards the house, finding some comfort in the only woman who could see me. And yet, as I stared up at the house, I could see the faint outlines of two or three people stood watching from the upstairs windows. Perhaps they were the children, the family that Mrs Price had spoken so fondly of, or previous owners who had bore witness to the changes in the house over the years. And Mrs Price herself, who seemed almost transparent in this light, was she of this world? I resolved that I had endless time to find out as my feet kept moving towards the open door, a most unexpected and hidden resting place as I parted from one world to the next.

And that is how it happens. Life continues and one by one we all stop, like the missing hands of Mrs Price's clock, we melt away when it is our time, we become nothing more than whisperings and knocks within the walls. Tomorrow you will wake up in your dimension and there will still be a house for sale and there will be new buyers trying to make sense of strange footsteps and unknown faces. The walls will breathe and sigh with our memories and we will be the scars of all that has been, watching for all that is still to come.

THE PIER

Clevedon, 2009

It was as if the place had been frozen in time. The faint and familiar smell of saltwater hit his nostrils, as he edged along the hotel pathway, dragging his small but overfilled suitcase behind him. He panted slightly at the steep incline up to the hotel's front door, a zigzag of brick pathway and neat flowerbeds that led him, in the most orderly of fashions, up to the converted house.

He stopped to take in the view, once more, the pastel washed houses that stood in slanted rows, the bandstand, the iron railings that led down to the more treacherous beach walks, memories of his family, as a boy, came flooding back as he took in gulps of that seawater scent that blew along with the breeze. He had grown up here, this place had housed so many years of his childhood, the years that saw him become a young man that, all at once, he was almost sorry he had left.

"Hello?" he called out, as he squeezed himself through front door, the suitcase snapping on its wheels behind him.
He was expecting a reception full of people waiting, a friendly face behind the counter, but the room was empty. His voice echoed as he called again, stretching up to take in the two large oak staircases that led to a balcony overlooking the ground floor, which was tiled with black and white marble. It had a certain, tired grandeur about it, as if time had erased much of the merriment this hotel must have housed in its time.

He stepped further in, making his way to the reception counter where he had spotted a bell, noticing the yellowing spots of marble, from years of arriving and departing guests. The sound of his shoes clicked and echoed, masking the faint sound of music that could be heard. It must have been coming from the bar and restaurant area, he thought to myself, as the sound of approaching footsteps turned his attention to the left staircase.

"Mr James." Her voice was as staccato as her footsteps, keeping a firm and steady beat as her heels clicked down the wooden steps. As she got closer, he could see the glint of a silver nametag on her black blazer. She was dressed head to toe in black, a fitted black blouse under the blazer that was tucked into a tight-fitting black pencil skirt. He caught a whiff of a floral scent as she moved closer, behind the counter. "Mr James, I presume?"

"Oh, yes." He had forgotten to respond, intimidated by the school-mistress charm of the mysterious woman, whose name, according to her nametag, was Marion. "Sorry, I think I'm a little late, I got held up on the way out of London."

"No need to apologise, Mr James," she replied, her voice was softening a little, as she ticked his name off on a paper booking sheet and typed something into a computer, each movement robotic and precise. "I know how London can be. I'll just get your keys for you."

"Thank you very much," he replied. "Did you get the message I left a few nights ago? I am looking to prolong my stay for over a week now, if there is room?"

The woman looked back towards from the key cupboard, her fingers trickling along the numbers, to find the correct one. Her face softened into a half smile, her forehead creased, forming a faint ridge between her scraped back bun and her smooth red lips, cracked at the corners.

"It really is no problem, Mr James. As you can see, this is not high season for us, we will need to discuss payment arrangements – but they can wait until tomorrow, I imagine you'll be wanting to rest."

He followed Marion's hands as she gestured around the emptiness of the reception area.

"Well thank you, I appreciate it," he replied, "I'm trying to get a book written, well finished, actually. It might take me longer than a week."

"As soon as you know, Mr James, then let us know." She grabbed a set of keys and placed them on the counter, pushing them in his direction. "Room 44. It's on the first floor and, if I may say so, it has one of the best views from the hotel. Would you like me to help you with your luggage?"

"Oh, no," he replied, far too much of a gentleman to watch the woman struggle with his bulging suitcase. "Please don't worry yourself, it's just one flight of stairs."

And with that, he took the keys from the counter and reached down to grab the handle of his suitcase and wheel it to the winding staircase, still immersed in the eerie quiet of the building, the music he had heard was now completely inaudible.

"Although, while I think of it, is the restaurant still serving lunch? I could really do with something to eat."

"Were you not informed, Mr James?" Marion's reply was sharp again, business-like, as she replaced the pile of papers she had picked up from the desk.

"Informed of what?" he replied. "And please, call me Dan."

"The bar and restaurant are out of action for the first few days of your stay." Marion motioned to the bar entrance, the door was shut tight, with a 'Do Not Enter' sign hanging from it.

He struggled to recollect whether he had noticed the sign upon his arrival, lost in a timewarp of his childhood, he presumed.

"It's undergoing some, um, refurbishment, but we hope to re-open midweek. There are quite a few places to eat along here, shall I see if we have some menus available?"

"I see." Puzzled, he accepted the offer of menus, gripped the handle of his suitcase and made for the foot of the staircase again.

The two nodded a swift farewell, before he ascended the staircase and Marion immersed herself in her pile of paperwork. He stopped halfway up the stairs, his ears straining to hear the music again, but all remained in complete silence and, with nothing but the sound of treading feet and squeaking wheels for company, he made his way to Room 44.

* * *

The room was smaller than he had imagined. From the small brochure that the hotel staff had been kind enough to send him, each room looked sizeable, with large four poster beds and bay windows that overlooked the sea. The view from Room 44 was indeed impressive. Situated in the middle of the building, the large bay window looked out across the ocean and much of the town, as the road wound along the short promenade and up to the cliffs. Dan had often ridden his bike along the promenade, where the tired-looking carousel horses had strived along their permanent journeys and memories of toffee-smeared mouths and excited children carrying prize cuddly toys, would stretch out to his ascent into adulthood. He would often sneak out late at night as he got older, when there was nobody but the smatterings of older, bored youths parked on benches with cans of beer or grouped in the bandstand to offset the rain, the orange glow of cigarettes lighting their silhouettes, as he sped past on beloved BMX bike. He stood a while in the window, his mind collapsing into the hazy details of life as a boy; someone innocent, excitable, always looking for adventure. And for the first time since his late arrival, he remembered his old friend Johnny. A brief but clear memory of the two racing off along the cliffside. He shuddered, focusing back to the present, to the view and its old familiarities.

His eyes widened to the further horizons of the sea, where the misty blue of the water met with the greying clouds of the sky. A frame, a ghost stood in the water, the soft waves lapped around its embedded steel rods; the dilapidated shell of the pier. It had been a main attraction when he was growing up. He remembered the creak of the wooden floorboards as he had crossed the bridge to the amusements, often with his parents but, later, with Johnny. It all seemed so quaint now; distorted mirrored halls, the model fortune teller who would spit predictive pieces of paper out for a sum of pocket money. He had spent so many summers perusing the delights of the arcades, running back and forth for more money and more sweets from his parents, even staring at the glowing lights of the pier, the far-off sounds of people enjoying themselves, as he was sent to bed each night.
But that was all gone now. A grim skeleton of what it had once been, the pier stood sombre and alone, fighting the waves as they licked and tore at its roots, its bones. His body gave out another involuntary shudder as he gazed at the steel skeleton, wondering what happened to it, when everything else in the quaint town seemed to have been frozen in time. The neat rows of houses seemed almost unchanged, whitewashed and coloured bricks had barely eroded but faded, with time. The bandstand looked to have had a recent fresh lick of paint, the decorative floral patterns still vibrant against the ivy-green of its structure. But the pier, stood and watched from its tragic anchor out at sea, like someone lost or drowning. And as he stepped away from the window to unpack his suitcase, all he could think about was the endurance of time, of what he had been and what he had become. And if he listened very carefully, he could hear the sound of music, funfair music, the music that had ebbed from the lively thrill seekers at the pier, all those years ago.

***

It was still early when he awoke, dawn was breaking its way through shrouds of black and grey, as he crept over to the window to survey the view once more. His first night at the hotel had been largely uneventful, he had grabbed a semi-edible pizza from a local fast food restaurant and opted to take it back to his room, to try and finish writing. The clouds had darkened somewhat since his arrival, with the promise of rain, and he had craved shelter and comfort for the evening. Almost four lines into the final chapter, he had given up, his mind plagued with the events of the last few weeks. He had looked at his phone over again, wondering whether to make a phone call, talking himself out of it until, somewhere between the depths of midnight and 1 a.m., he admitted defeat, with his manuscript, with her and took to his bed.

He had been sleeping less and less during the last few weeks at home. The inevitable breakdown of his relationship had caused no end of stress, whilst his teaching job was winding down for the Christmas holidays and he had begun to feel trapped in the same job he had done for years. The trip back to Clevedon had been suggested by his manager, who saw the advance of tired lines and greying hair, who had been privy to the problems in his personal life. Between them both, they had hoped it would give him breathing space and clarity, so far it had made him long to be a boy again, to relinquish all the responsibilities he had stacked up since his departure. But it was early days, and it had been no shock to see his phone screen winking 4.30 a.m. as he rolled over to check the time. Or to check for messages from her.

He had grown accustomed to the stillness of the early mornings, each movement he made seemed almost secretive, against the silence of the rest of the world. Resolving to give in to his body clock, he forced himself from the bed and made a small coffee from the complimentary amenities in the hotel room. The white plastic kettle appeared to vibrate as it bubbled to boiling point, he poured it into the plain white mug and wandered over to the window.

Stillness. There was something so desolate, so deafening about the morning. In London, an early morning walk would have greeted another late-night straggler – London was a city that never truly slept. But here, there was not another soul, as far as the eye could see, perhaps the faint glimmer of lights on in some varied houses, across near the cliffs. Early starts for the day, shift workers, but the pavements were dead, he could not even hear the cries and squawks of seagulls, or any birds, overhead.

He was drawn over to the pier again, looming from its watery grave, its steel structure blackened against the darkness of the early morning. He allowed those childhood memories to swarm over him, for just a second, before Johnny's picture emblazoned across his mind again and he almost dropped the hot coffee down himself.

Colours. He remembered vivid colours; the bright, blurred string lights of the pier shaping into view, as the two boys had sped along the seafront, dodging near accidents on the way. He remembered Johnny's bike, a bright red BMX, which shimmered as Johnny had wheeled it across the wooden planks, creaking them towards the magic out at sea. He remembered how envious he had been of that bike; his had been an older model, sturdy but dull and rusting a little at the wheels, dirty from constant use and no intention of cleaning. He had been like any boy creeping on the borders of teenage-hood, looking in from the smeared windows, he had cared so little for his belongings, always laughing at Johnny as he cleaned and preened his beloved bike almost daily. He closed his eyes, almost against the memories that were seeping back into his mind, colourful memories against an otherwise grey childhood, memories that time and place had allowed him to forget.

A light in the distance brought him back to his senses. His coffee cup, still in his hand, was wavering now, unsteady as his eyes were drawn back to a strange light glimmering from the direction of the pier. Yellow, golden at first, but it seemed to change quickly to red, to green and back to gold. It was warm, shapeless, almost unnoticeable at first, but it appeared to be emanating from the pier itself, colours set against the cold ink-like darkness of the early morning. He was unsure what he felt about it, other than mesmerised, as he continued to stare for the longest time. He snapped only when he heard the vibrating buzz of his mobile phone as it danced along the bedside table. Catching his breath, he walked over to check it. An alarm, no message, not at this time of the morning, although the clock now blinked 6.30 a.m. at him, he had whiled away two hours lost in consciousness. A wave of exhaustion crashed over him and the crumpled, unmade bed became too inviting all of a sudden. Placing his cup at the bedside table, he collapsed back under the covers, promising another hour before his day started. And yet, when sleep overcame him again, he was lost in vivid dreams of Johnny and a strange painted face that called his name.

***

Much of his first full day in Clevedon was spent hiding from the torrential downpours that had arrived overnight. Though as much as he hated the perpetual damp of British winter, there was also something beautiful about the town and the way that it smelled in the rain; fresh and earthy.

He had taken a stroll out at about 11.30 a.m. after a much-needed rest, although he had been awoken by Marion banging loudly on his door, with the offer of tea and toast, in the absence of the open hotel restaurant. He had accepted the toast gladly, he was exhausted and hungry after his early morning rouse, whilst Marion invited herself in, presumably to inspect the room. She had been dressed in her uniform of black again, a dress this time, though still starched and fitted. He made a silent acknowledgment of her strange beauty, whilst she talked about the re-opening of the restaurant and the new head chef who had proposed a fantastic new menu – by her account. He had listened eagerly, whilst suppressing the uneasy feeling of being watched in his room by unseen eyes, he could not fathom his feelings or even what they were; only that he felt a sense of discomfort. Or foreboding.

Once he had dressed and tidied up his bed, being careful to overlook his laptop with a pang of guilt, he grabbed an old raincoat he had thrown into his suitcase and decided to take a walk around his old hometown. He was somewhat relieved to pass two new guests checking in, as he descended the stairs by the reception, nodding a greeting as he headed for the main doors. Perhaps that would ease his discomfort, not feeling so alone in the hotel, he smiled to himself as he shook off his uneasiness and propped up an umbrella, to protect himself from the downpour.

Once he was outside in the rain, he worked out his bearings, opting to take a walk against the flurry of the rainfall, towards the beach, though the pull of the pier – which was now closed off to the general public, swayed him as he chose his direction. He breathed in the fresh air, tinged with sea salt and faintly familiar smells of candyfloss and colourful, sweet treats – unless that was his imagination awakening again; years spent living and working in central London had hardened his lungs to the constant pollution and smoke.

He walked along the promenade that was still almost deserted, as the grey day promised to bring more bad weather. He stopped to take shelter under the bandstand when the showers became heavier, just moments after he left the comfort of his hotel. The first buds of spring were beginning to break through the bitter cold of the winter, blooms of colour would replace the drab, grey feel of the walk soon enough. He secretly hoped he would still be here to see it. One week would not be long enough to finish the final chapters, to clear his head of the emotional fog that he left behind in London. And he had still heard nothing from her, no request for news of his safe arrival, no updates, she had not even wanted to know how he was. He looked out to the sea, the veil of rain showers now dissipating to a fine mist; he wanted to feel like he was home. But this was not home, this had not been home since... since he had left.

***

He found a cosy café tucked inside a holiday caravan and ordered a hot, strong coffee and a bacon sandwich. The deceptive rain had picked up on his walk along the promenade, even a glimpse of the waves crashing against the cliff edges made him think twice about venturing too far. He dove inside for comfort and dryness, whilst the town remained desolate and somewhat silent.

He remembered the beach, brimming with sunbathing lizards and playful families, as a child; his own family would often head there during the summer as soon as the warm weather hit. They only lived a stone's throw from the town, they would traipse down with beach balls and towels, cool bags packed with jam sandwiches and diluted orange squash. How he was scolded when he tried to take his BMX bike without permission, how he would spend hours playing frisbee with unfamiliar school children, whilst his mum read her book in the heat of the sun. Those were special memories, untainted and untouched by the discomfort and the horrors of his teenage years. Another involuntary shudder shot through him, as he swigged the last dregs of his coffee from the polystyrene cup and wrapped his damp coat around him, determined to head back to the hotel to write; the pull of the pier pierced through him again, as he remembered the strange, colourful glow that he had seen that morning. Shaking his head, he pulled his hood up as tightly as he could and vacated his seat, heading back along the same stretch of road.

He was almost back at the hotel when he heard the first, distant roll of thunder, preceded by a sudden shock of lightning. The sky had darkened, ink-black on his short walk, though he had been so lost in his thoughts and in the scenery to notice, the fork of lightning hit somewhere in the distance, illuminating the abandoned grey matter of the pier.

Somewhere, in his memory, he remembered standing at this exact spot, perhaps his bike had been rested against the sandstone barrier, perhaps the sky had been lighter, less blackened but still thundering. He remembered standing at this exact spot with his camera, his precious possession that he had begged his parents for one Christmas, when he was almost thirteen, the camera that then became permanently strapped around his neck at every opportunity. The waves had looked much as they did now, foaming and rippling as the tide played with the wind. Only across the shore, the pier would still have been full of some life, some promise of rides and treats and thrills to come. And as he reached into his pocket for his phone, the only digital item he now carried with him, desperate to snap the danger and beauty in this moment, he remembered how he had struggled to find the pier through his viewfinder, in the deepening darkness, how he had been distracted by the glowing lights that were emanating from the pier, blues, golds and greens, and how he had clicked away at the same spot, hoping for a good shot to show his parents, or his art teacher at school. And as the man had stood in that same spot, his hands frozen and clasped around the tiny phone, its focus flickering in the gathering storm, he had remembered the day that the photos were developed. He had remembered the blackness of the photos, each one showing an outline of the pier structure, but the essence of the storm had not been captured, the heart of his art had been lost. Except for one frame, one shot of a tall figure, light, wisped as if he was almost not there, skulking in the shadows of the closed pier, his loose clothing and ruff in full silhouette against the black of the image. The image of a clown was staring back at him, through the photo, from the pier; a clown who had not been there at all.

***

The sound stirred him from a doze, awakening both the boy he had been and the man he now was. It was faint, at first, as if blowing on the sea breeze itself, its gentle whirring was almost knocking against the thin panes of the hotel window; an unfamiliar room in an all-too familiar place, as the events of the day came flooding back to him.

The mechanical winding of a dreamscape music box scraped across his brain as he shook himself awake, feeling along the side of his bed for his phone, the blurred red lines of an alarm clock formed into stark digits. 01.00. His body cocooned back into the warmth of the bed, his hand tucked back under the quilts, fighting a chill that ran across him.

The whirring music, like an old-fashioned music box still played to itself, somewhere in the distance. It seemed closer than before, perhaps the rain had softened, flecking against his window as he pulled his covers up and feigned another attempt to sleep. It had thundered late into the evening; rain had threatened its way in from the east, the clouds had continued to gather and taunt above the shell of the pier. He had run back to the hotel, dodging a passing car that had sped around the corner, its lights blurring his vision as he darted across to shelter, frightened from the memory of his strange photographs and the image that had shown in development. He had snapped down on his phone button several times, he had not known why; only that the power of his memories upon his return here had already unearthed things that he would rather have stayed hidden, buried.

He had even found Marion to be on an afternoon off, once he was safely inside the confines of the hotel. He had had the briefest thought to sit with her for an hour or two, to calm himself down. Instead he was greeted by an unknown face on reception – a younger man named David, whose pleasantries and brief anecdotes on the weather could not stir Dan from his fear, fear that showed across his lined face and exhausted body. There had been a reason for his leaving here after all, it had not just been the stuff of long-forgotten nightmares.

Once inside his room, he had flicked the switch and closed all the curtains, not wishing to take in the sea view anymore, only haunted by the photographs he had long forgotten about. He sat on the edge of the bed, taking no notice of the wet clothes he still had on, the rain still dripping down his back from the downpour. He fumbled in his inner pocket for his phone, for evidence that his mind was playing tricks on him. He wiped the smooth surface of the screen, dotted in raindrops, now smeared with his handprints and punched in his code, ignoring his shaking fingers as he did so. He searched for the 'photos' icon on his phone, pressing gently against its colourful logo and swiping through the blackened images. And his phone dropped to the side of the bed as he came across one stark image, the sea of blackness almost enveloping the familiar shape of an entity, long dead, much like the pier itself, staring back at him, through his phone, across the waves and almost across time itself.

***

He closed his eyes, the music swimming through him, as he remembered lights and people, the crowds of tall people that he and Johnny would dart through on their BMXs, desperate to get to the amusements before anyone else. How the lights would shimmer on the lapping water, swaying in the soft breeze of a Summer's evening, enticing the small crowds to the penny arcades and circus shows. Primitive, to some, but to him it was the most magical time of the year. The shell of the pier, gloomy and abandoned in its watery mausoleum, brought to life.

His memories played out like a film, the strange soundtrack provided a perfect setting, as he watched his boyhood self, in his mind's eye, soak up the wonders of the travelling show, memories etched and now tarnished, as he remembered the crunch of a toffee apple, so heavy on its wooden stick that he could barely support it. The music played, louder still, the wind was whipping up and battering against the side of the hotel. But it was the distinct sound of a knock that made him sit, bolt upright in bed. He heard it once, twice and a third time, against the window pane. This did not have the imperfect patterns of hard, pelting raindrops, but the distinct and certain knocking of knuckles on glass.

And then he remembered.

The clown. Not the fluffy, playful clowns of children's parties with water pistol flower tricks and oversized feet. This had been the stuff of his nightmares, exaggerated in his trauma, he knew not if it had been human or some other entity, a man clad in a thick mask of face paint, his putrid breath pungent in the boy's nostrils. His outfit was worn and greying, frayed around the edges and made from layers of a shiny cotton, creased and broken. A soft striped ruff, ripped and torn at the edges, sat under his chin, drenched in spittle, with burn holes that resembled eye sockets nestled in between the layers of fabric.

He screwed his nose up as the memory wisped through his mind, patchy, warped, as if the fingers of his mind were struggling to grasp the edges, as if waking from a dream, its premise on the tip of his tongue, the details long forgotten. Like the shape in the photo images, he or it was blurred, it shifted, almost floated through space, but he knew now that the thing had most definitely been there.

And still, the music played, both faint and yet almost as if it played in the same room, at the same time. The faint knocking returned, less of a gap between them now, more with an urgency. He sat up in bed, dread creeping from his legs upwards, freezing him to the spot, nestled around the bedclothes.

Johnny.

***

"Help!" He heard Johnny cry.

A memory skated through him, he had found Johnny lying at the bottom of the stairs at school one bright, summer's evening. Tim Morrish was Johnny's neighbour and the school bully. A towering, thin boy, Morrish was the stuff of early secondary school nightmares, too much mouth and not enough to do with it, productively. Johnny had been his target from the first day of school; hunting him down on journeys home, stealing lunch money and making idol threats – or so it had seemed – until the day he pushed Johnny down the stairs. Danny did not know what to do, their friendship was new, fresh and he knew nothing of Johnny's trauma with Morrish and his band of tag-a-long bullies. He did the right thing, helping Johnny to his feet and dusting off his backpack, he walked home with him that afternoon, even though it meant a fifteen-minute detour, the boy was limping; his left ankle had been crushed upon his fall – though no permanent damage was done.

"I'll get them." Johnny would murmur throughout their journey, his face screwed up in anger, his eyes small and cursing as he regaled Danny with his stories of Morrish's early attempts to threaten and scare him.

"Anyway," he would continue, "I've got someone on my side, someone who has promised me that they're gonna get 'em for me."

"Who?" Danny had replied, confused as to who would be so bold to stand sides with the much smaller, quainter Johnny. "Lewis?"

Johnny had stopped in his tracks, as if he were about to release a secret to the world, he had been tentative, unsure as to whether or not Danny was worthy of his knowledge.

"Not Lewis, not anyone from school…Charlie."

And in that moment, though he knew nothing about Charlie, nor did he recognise the name from anywhere, he felt the attack of a chill race down his spine, as if something had been unleashed upon him too.

***

"Help!" Another memory surfaced. Johnny had been shorter than him, more slight. Tougher with his words now – spouting hatred at Tim Morrish as he had cornered them at least once a week for six months, demanding lunch money or just the opportunity to throw punches.

Danny – Dan – was taller, his shoulders burgeoning into the broad outline of the man he would later become, was quieter, unprotective, unresponsive to most. Even though they were the best of friends, Danny and Johnny barely spoke to each other. They lived through their summers without the complication of unnecessary words, they spoke when they needed to – arranging times and places, necessary snacks and finding new bike trails – and then they would head off together, alone, with only their trusty bike steeds and an air of silence that nobody could penetrate, only the laughter that broke through on occasion. Johnny was quiet, Danny liked that, though he never knew why. It had been nine months since he had helped Johnny home after his fall down the staircase, since he had revealed the name of an unknown assailant, the words had not crossed Johnny's lips again. Though there had been trips to the pier in the heat of the summer holidays, where Johnny had seemingly disappeared to find something or someone. Danny had never questioned it and, like any thirteen year old boy, did not waste his time on small talk, where there was fun to be had. Only that was the same year that Danny had captured the strange image on his camera, the image of the clown that had been watching him from his watery home.

The Pier was opening for the summer holidays, the rainy spring season was coming to an end, as was the school year. Johnny and Danny sat in their usual comfortable silence, as gaggles of school children talked excitedly of their summer plans. Some were heading abroad for the holidays in the sun, others would be visiting family in the country. Most would be making a trip to the pier at least once. Johnny and Danny silently contemplated the long stretch of six weeks ahead of them. For them, there would be multiple bike rides and trips to the pier, days out walking along the beach and chances for Danny to practice with his new camera. For them, they were coming of age; now that they were teenagers, both Danny and Johnny's parents had allowed them to go to the pier amusements and the beach on their own. There were stringent rules and talk of what would happen if one of them got lost, the importance of sticking together and the rule of not staying out past dusk, but whatever the consequences were, they were going to experience freedom for the first time, the usual antics of the two that were no longer going to be watched by the all-seeing eyes of their parents, near or far. And for that, neither boy could wait.

The pier opened its amusements to the public again a week after school had finished for the year. The suspense had been unbearable for Danny and Johnny, who had had to make do with milder temperatures and intermittent rain showers all week. The arrival of the pier's familiar lights and music also signalled a heatwave for the residents of the town, the population had gathered on the narrow, creaking promenade for its opening day.

At 5p.m. Danny and Johnny rode their bikes across the decking, dodging the crowds of people, coins and notes bulging their pockets ready to spend on treats and arcade games. They had exhausted all the money that they had by 7p.m., not stopping for something good to eat or a break to take in the view, the adrenalin had pushed them to spend and not savour. And so, with empty pockets and hungry tummies, they walked their bikes back along the promenade, stopping only when Johnny jumped around, as if called by someone.

Tim Morrish. And his band of misfits, grouped together behind the two boys, they stood, bikes like steeds, penknives like swords, glinting and threatening in the sun, the boys carried crooked smiles and hideous promises and, before, the boys could make a decision, the bikes began to edge towards them.

The boys rode as fast as their BMX's could carry them, pedalling at such speed, hurtling past the crowds who were seemingly unaware of the danger that the boys were facing, it crossed Danny's mind to cry for help, uncertain of what that would mean for them if Morrish heard. Johnny, who was about half a metre head, turned to nod at Danny, Danny nodded back, they were going to head for the woods behind the cliffs, where they knew they could lose Morrish and his crowd at the thickest part and hide out for a while until it was safe to pedal home to their parents. Johnny skidded his bike to a halt, as a figure loomed into view in front of them.

At first glance he appeared to be floating, levitating along the decking, the tips of battered shoes, mostly hidden under large, bunched trousers of the same material, dragging in silence across the wooden boards, he was moving towards them, his face twisted into a gruesome smile, the chalked white smeared across his face, nestled into deep lines. The boys were frozen in fear, yet the crowds surrounding them seemed to be none the wiser to the appearance of this shape, the clown with the bloody mouth and the beckoning finger. It was as if only Johnny and Danny could see him, or react to him, even Morrish's lot seemed unaware of why their prey had stopped dead on the promenade. And just like that, the strange being, the gruesome apparition, disappeared into nothing but a ball of light, golds, blues and reds hovered and shimmered above their heads, as they pedalled for their lives through the small town and out towards the woods, with Morrish and his clan swift on their tails.

The chaos of the pier crowds and the evening revellers scattered along the beach, soon disappeared to nothing more than the sounds of screeching metal and the boys panting heavily against the incline of the hill. They had been confident that they would know their way through the woods better than Morrish, following the hypnotic light as it bounced above them, trusting their instincts to pull off into a thicket to swerve away from the enemies, seemingly guided by the orb of light, the shapeshifting clown whose appearance had been so frightening. Johnny led up ahead, his bike newer and faster, the brakes more powerful as he hurtled towards a sudden left turning that both boys were aware of, from their constant travels.

A swift swerve, but not to the left, to the right, Danny watched as Johnny began to lose control of his bike, not stopping to contemplate Johnny's movements he followed, not wanting to be left behind to face Morrish alone, but scared to follow onto the unknown path. As he swerved, Danny and his bike fell apart, he felt the solid wheels fall from under him as he landed on a softened pile of dirt and grass. He scrambled to his feet, to be met with silence, only the uncontrollable spin of the wheel spokes could be heard, not even Morrish's crew made a sound of approach. Staying cautious, he lifted his bike to a standing position and wheeled it along the path, being careful not to trip over the growing stumps of trees and low-lying branches.

"Help!" He heard his friend try to scream. He stood still, the blood rushing down to his feet as he became paralysed. There was only one or two trees between him and the terrifying scene. Johnny's bright red bike was slumped on the ground, whilst he had been lifted high in the air, arms and legs flailing as the hideous being clasped his huge hands around his neck, his lined face closing in on Johnny, drinking in the expression of terror on the boy's face as he took one deep breath in and appeared to suck the very life from Johnny. Danny watched in horror, unable to make a sound as his friend went limp in the grip of the monster that had lured them away from the pier, each limb swung to a stop, his terrified eyes closed, his neck stiffened as the clown breathed in the last of Johnny before swinging his lifeless body over the clifftop, like a ragdoll being hurled to a deep, watery grave. Without another word, or a glance to find the other boy, Danny, concealed within the bushes and scared to the very bone, the clown disappeared before his very eyes.

And it was nightfall before anybody found the terrified child and the abandoned scarlet BMX, by the clifftop.

***

He was sweating now, as his long-forgotten story washed over him, triggered by the appearance of the strange figure who had lured or even followed Johnny and Danny into the woods that day. Danny had almost forgotten about Charlie before he appeared to them on the promenade, Johnny had looked uncomfortable but also knowing at the same time. He had encountered the being before, he had spoken of his promise to protect him from Morrish, yet he seemed to have made a deal with the Devil himself, his protection, in turn became his untimely exit from this world.

Echoes of laughter ran through him, like sonic polaroids, he could almost feel the beating heat of the sun as it had bore down on their ruddy, tanned necks as they skidded and pedalled along dirt tracks, exploring new places in a place where nothing was new.

Knock Knock.

He resisted the urge to shout, 'who is there?', succumbing to the victim state in every bad horror film he had ever watched, choosing to forget the scenes he had experienced in real time.
"Help!"
The sound ran through him again, John's voice, gargled and disembodied, he no longer knew if the echo was in his mind or if the voice that rang out was really that of John. He nestled in again, his hands fumbling on the side table for earphones, his phone, anything that would block out the sounds that he was still pretending not to hear. He felt the loose, cool wire, draped across the table and pulled it towards him, followed by his phone, careful to place it under the covers before the screen lit up. He did not know why, whoever was knocking, was aware that he was there.

Knock

The phone lit up, his fingers punched in the four digit code – the anniversary of his now-defunct marriage, or so he assumed. He clicked the earphones into place and scrolled down his list of music, to find something soothing, all the while his hands were shaking. And he froze in terror, as the familiar drone of the old music box blasted through his headphones.

He ripped the phones from his ears, pulling on the lobes in the process and wincing at the dull ache left behind. He could still hear the distant sound of the music as it streamed through the phones, now lying defunct on the floor.

All these years, Dan had suppressed the memories of Clevedon, of his shameful walk home, once the police had found him cowering in the thicket, his face hot with streams of tears, muddy knees and no explanation. Of course his parents assumed that he had been unable to save his friend from an unfortunate fall, they would not have been able to comprehend the horror of what he had witnessed and how he did nothing to save his friend from such a grisly death. In the wake of Johnny's death, Morrish's clan had crumbled under the pressure too, each choosing different areas of the schoolyard to hang out. He presumed that they too had blamed themselves for the death, though he never looked in their direction again. Within six months, Danny's parents had taken the difficult decision to leave the town, opting for somewhere on the outskirts of London, for job security, or so they said. Then began several months of psychotherapy for Danny, who missed his friend so dearly. But Charlie's work was done, Johnny had been protected, in exchange for his very soul.

A rattle. The sound of the doorknob as it twisted on its hinge, he felt his breathing deepen, become heavy as if fear itself was resting on his chest. Whatever was trying to get into the room would not stop, would not rest until they had made their presence known. He had come back to be claimed.

The wind was still howling, knocking against the windows, threatening, as the door handle continued to rattle. He no longer knew what were memories and what was happening in the present, he thought he heard a voice, child-like and lost, calling out his name, but he shut his eyes and willed whatever was trying to break in to be gone. Be gone or stop taunting him. The last thing he remembered was letting out an almighty scream as the bulk of a shadow moved across the bottom of his bed, shapeless and swaying like trees in the wind, and the scream protruded from his lungs until he lost consciousness.

***

The alarm clock jolted him awake the next morning. He sat bolt upright in bed, feeling his face and back drenched in sweat. He could not recall falling asleep, only the faint memory of needing to pick his phone off the floor, but being frozen to the spot. Daylight brought with it some calm and restoration to the room. The thunderstorm had ceased overnight, leaving an eerie but bright quiet start to the morning. He looked around the room, the curtains were still half-drawn, the door still locked and whoever had been trying to enter his room the night before had not. There had been no physical manifestation, perhaps it had all replayed in his mind, his brain washing over childhood memories. He was only certain of one thing, at this moment, that he needed to vacate his room, to vacate the town as soon as possible. With that thought, he set about packing his bags and dressing in crumpled clothing.

Tomorrow would bring another day, another round of writing and deleting, losing the words on the tip of his tongue and of fighting the urge to call his wife. For now, he would drift off, dreamless and helpless. And nobody would be any wiser about the old story of the boys that disappeared into the woods, as they followed the wispy silhouette of a clown, a clown that they had seen dragging himself on the pier; a misted entity of laughter and of fear, that they had been running from something. They would not know that curiosity had got the better of Johnny and that he had become tangled in the taunts and hauntings of 'Charlie', that they had followed the tendrils of his blackened soul as he reaped his way through the secluded woods, wrapping himself through the crooked trees and luring him to the blackest and most dangerous thicket. And that one boy made it out alive and that one boy didn't, and that the elusive man who had come to stay in his old home town for the week, was the only person who knew the true horror of those events and the gruesome ghost who had murdered his friend.

He settled his bill with Marion at the reception, citing work as a reason to end his stay so abruptly, not wishing to spend another moment in this haunted place, or in his haunted head. It may have been his imagination, but he sensed some disappointment from Marion as he signed the last sheet. She bade him farewell in her professional tone, though he spun around in surprise as she called out to him,
"I heard some…commotion last night, from your room." She had heard him, his scream perhaps. "Was everything alright?"
"Oh, yes," he stifled a reply, wishing to remain aloof until he was safely away from the town, "night terrors, always had 'em, since I was a kid."

"How awful." Marion replied. "You know, Dan, you should make a trip back here in the summer."

"Yes, maybe I will, not the weather for it at the moment." He had absolutely no intention of returning.

"Rumour has it, the pier is undergoing work again." Her mention of it sent a chill through his spine. "It's going to re-open in the summer."

"Well…thank you, for that." he replied.

"Safe journey…Dan." Her smile had a knowingness that chilled his blood, he bolted for the door and the safety of his car, unwilling to let any more of his story unravel.

The rain that had subsided had started trickling again, flecks appeared on his windscreen as he fumbled with his car keys to start the engine. He breathed a sigh of relief as the car sprung to life, the familiar lights danced into action along the dashboard, although his eyes were, once more, drawn to the skeleton of the pier, still visible through the low fog. Perhaps he just needed to remember, he thought to himself, pushing the horrible memories away, not wishing to linger on the things that happened to him so long ago, but wishing to acknowledge Johnny and his gruesome demise at the hands of something from a horror film. And yet, if he squinted, he could still make out the soft glow of a light in the distance. Reds, blues, golds and greens danced their way across the metal bars of the huge, stranded structure, perhaps ready for new victims that coming summer. And as he drove off, back to the confines of smog and desperation, of an unknown future with or without his wife and with new memories freshly aroused from the pits of his mind in which they had been locked for so long. And along the way, the music…still played.

A BAG OF SOULS

I am afraid of the dark. It's a strange thing, really. I wasn't afraid as a child. I had a tendency to wander at night, back when I was a girl. I was always restless under covers, feet itching to move and explore. I had no sense of time, no need for sleep, I wanted to see more of the world and feel its magic, cloaked beneath the night sky. Do you believe in magic? I did, I believed in it all, fairies and hags and princesses, lifted from the pages of the endless story books and fairy tales I would indulge in. I believed that the twists of tales could reach out into our own world, that only if you believed, you could see.

I would squeeze my eyes shut so tight, that the backs of my lids would hurt, in anticipation of what was out there in the shadows, willing to fool my parents as they lulled themselves into a night time routine. I would wait until my parents were both fast asleep, lying patiently under my covers, until the click of the last light switch would plunge the house into darkness. I would feel across the mattress for the miniature torchlight that I kept hidden underneath the covers, slipping my feet out from under the duvet, I would inch them along the floor until they felt upon the soft sheepskin lining of my slippers.

Keeping the flashlight low against my hip, I would creep along the hallway, careful to disguise any creak of a floorboard as I did. I would sometimes stumble over the cat, as she lay splayed out across the landing, a hurdle between me and my midnight freedom, her furry body stretched out towards the staircase. Over the months and years that my secret wanderings had become commonplace, I had perfected the placement of each step to ensure my exit from the house remained unknown. Looking back, I must have left the house at least twenty times and really, I wasn't leaving the house at all. I only ever went wandering in the back garden. Until that night, anyway.

Once I was outside, I would revel in the dampness of the evening, feeling the dewy grass as it splattered against my slippers. The streetlights would flicker in the dim moonlight, casting a glow over my midnight activities. I would watch, wait, wander, planning adventures and hoping for a glimpse of something beautiful, magical, something not of this world. But, mostly, I would stare into the depths of twilight and try to find my place in the world, childhood was fast leaving me behind and I wasn't sure I was ready to let go, not at that time. I would long for an accomplice, another midnight friend with whom I could make plans with, I would go to the end of our garden, slip onto the upturned wooden pallet that had lay disused for so long, and stare over the wall into the backs of our neighbours' gardens, hoping to find another me wishing and wandering for the very same things.

On that particular night, I remember it was getting colder, a soft breeze was blowing around my dressing gown; it had a bite to it, a reminder that the winter months were fast approaching. I had successfully escaped the confines of my bedroom and the house, without disturbing the cat and keeping the flashlight to a minimum as I crept out to my favourite hiding place, under the stars. A light rain had fallen earlier that evening, its droplets still lingering on the plants scattered around our garden, readying themselves for their winter shed. I heard a noise at the bottom of the garden, its sound echoed through my spine in a shiver. A rustle, at first, followed by the scrape of a boot or shoe as if it was trying to climb the brick wall. I held up my flashlight and ran, without thinking, towards the end of our garden. My eyes caught the hulking figure of a shape as it bounded on top of the wall, its foot seemed to be caught in something, as it scraped and pulled to get free. Afraid, but curious, I shone my flashlight directly in the face of my startled intruder.

A boy, not much older than me, his eyes were wide with terror, his hair was short and matted, his features were dark from what I could tell in the dim light. He was crouched on the top of the red brick wall that blocked the end of my garden from the alleyway that snaked between the rows of houses, still trying to free his right foot from the wire trapping along the wall; his hands were pressing hard into the rough brick. He looked distorted, somehow, as if he was bent out of shape.

I lifted my torch again, to get a better look at his face, still nobody I recognised from the streets; he wasn't one of the boys who I would often dodge as they carelessly kicked about together, alone, in the alleyways and park entrances after school. His body, though hunched in the pitch black of night, appeared young, but his face under the harsh, luminous beam of my torch was lined, sunken; the boy looked as if he had lived one hundred years.

"Please," the boy spoke, his voice raspy, as if he was running out of air. "I don't want to hurt you. I'm trying to get away."

"From who?" I replied, my voice was calm, although inside I was frightened by the stranger and even more so by his strange face. As I looked more intently upon him, I could see patterns of grey lines appear in his jet-black mop of hair.

"They call him 'Reginald Rasper'." the boy replied, his voice had lowered to an almost whisper, in case of any disturbance. I moved in closer, reaching out to help release him from the trap – an old wire knot that once housed a long-forgotten birdfeeder. The wall was low enough for me to see over from almost waist-height on the pallet, so the boy and I were almost at equal head height now. I still found his aged face disconcerting, as I released his foot I noticed the tear in his shorts, my hand brushing against his soft adolescent skin.

A noise, a rustle from somewhere further down the street that echoed through the silence of the night and made the boy jump out of his skin. His sunken eyes darted back to me, not wishing to utter another word until he was safe. Without thinking, I proffered a hand to help him down from the wall and, in a blanket of silence with nothing but the dripping of a threatening rain shower, I led the strange creature towards the comfort of my home.

Once inside, I turned the lowest of lamps on, continually putting my finger to my lips, to warn the boy not to wake my parents,

"They will send you straight out, if they find you here." I warned him, though I was more concerned with what they would do to me. I settled the boy into an armchair in the furthest corner of the living room, fetching a glass of water and making sure each door and window was locked as I did so. Whatever, or whoever the boy was running from, had sent that inexplicable chill through my body.

It took me a few moments to coax the boy to speak, in this low lighting I could now see more grey hairs appearing in his matted hair, I shook my head at the notion that they were growing as I looked at him, but there did seem to be more appearing in small, think clumps. He took a gulp of water, his sullen eyes were staring at me all the while.

"Where do you live?" I began, logical with a means to finding this boy's way home before my parents caught wind of our midnight intruder. "What's your name?"

"Pardon me." His voice still trembled as he formed the words, he placed the glass on a small side table next to the armchair. "My name is Scott Saunders. I live at 14, Westwood Avenue. At least, I think I do."

"You think you do?" Confusion had spread across his face like the lines around his eyes. The skin across his face, around his cheeks looked fragile, stretched, skeletal.

"I do," His voice slowed as he soothed himself into the back of the armchair. "Tonight, feels like a few hours and a hundred years all at once, rolled into one. I just wanted to get back home."

I sat in silence, opposite, he looked ethereal somehow, as if a light surrounded him.

"I'm sorry to have woken you." He took another gulp of water, his wrists weak and barely able to hold the tumbler in one hand.

"Oh, you didn't." I smiled encouragingly. "I often take a walk out to my garden at night, I love the peace and quiet."

"Then you must stop." He raised his voice. "Whatever you do, don't stay out in the dark, on your own. They say he knows, they say he comes for those who wander."

"Who is...HE?" I replied, feeling the blood drain from my face as the boy gave out his warning. And, slowly, the boy leaned forward, his back hunched, not like before, but as if his skeleton was changing, deforming in front of me; he told me the story of Reginald Rasper.

"Once, long ago, there lived a man who was accused of kidnapping the local children. There was spate of children who went missing and everyone thought it was the work of the strange man they called Reginald The Rasper. He was an odd-looking sort of man, old and hunched at the shoulders with yellow crooked teeth, like fangs, and always dressed in odd mismatched suits. He got his name from his terrible rasping, a life-long condition that had left him with barely any voice, he wheezed when trying to speak; his words would form in the back of his throat and then he would spit them out with frustration and venom. The local people had always taken an instant dislike to him, with his quiet nature and looks picked straight from the page of a fairy tale. He became the ogre, the giant, the creature of nightmares, the warning that made all children behave. And yet, all that was known of him was that he would carry with him a bag, a burlap sack drawn tight at the top, that would sit across his shoulder bump against his crooked legs on the rare occasions that he was spotted out walking. With their disdain for Rasper, the towns people would speculate what he carried in the bag – one said he had heard a single, terrifying scream echo from it, when Rasper opened it within his earshot once. A Bag of Souls, they thought he was a soul collector, sent from the devil to claim souls bound for hell. And so it will come as no surprise that the increasing cases of the five missing children were blamed on Reginald but, with no evidence and I suspect a little bit of fear to stop the law intervening, Reginald was free to roam the town, scaring its residence with his cold stare and shaking silence.

Months passed and still, there was no sign of the missing children or clue as to what happened to them. One of the poor fathers had always remained hopeful that his daughter would return – he claimed to see her everywhere, that she appeared to him often at night, mouthing words to him that he could not hear. One night, when the breeze was starting to turn and the trees were bowing to shed their summer leaves, the grieving father was seen skulking in the shadows, wandering towards the tiny, desolate cottage that Rasper lived in at the edge of the town. He had been carrying something, he had been following the mirage of his lost daughter, or so he said, as she darted in between houses and trees and danced on the road. And he knocked on Rasper's door in the dead of night, banging with his fist, his eyes cold and his heart determined to find answers, and when Rasper refused to answer his door for the fourth time, the man set the tiny cottage on fire and watched as the flames licked and tore the cottage and its inhabitant to the ground."

"Was Rasper ever found?" I interrupted the boy's story. Even as I had been listening, spellbound, to the legend, his eyes had grown darker still, he looked as if he was wasting away.

"No, I believe they found scraps of clothing, enough to assume that Reginald had perished in the fire." he replied, lifting a skeletal hand to inspect as he did so. "The father was charged and imprisoned, he angered the people of the town because, of course, by burning down the cottage he removed any trace of possible evidence that Rasper had been responsible for the missing children. The mystery was never solved."

"So what happened to you?" I was direct, something about the corners of his mouth turning downwards, his hands that were now barely skin and bone, even his voice had grown weary, suggested that his time was growing short.

The boy coughed, a look of terror returned as his eyes widened, he continued on.

"I had always known about the story of Reginald and his bag of souls. My parents would tell me the story, the same as their parents had done. In the years that followed the tragedy, there would be stories of missing children, as well as adults too on occasion, who would simply disappear. Some would appear to be taken from their very beds, others would wave their parents goodbye, never to be seen again. There were no clues left to follow, nobody had seen them, no scents or trails to lead to them. It was as if they disappeared. And for those who knew the tale of Rasper and his gruesome death, there were whispers that he had come back to exact his revenge.

I thought it was nothing more than a tale, something to scare children back to their beds or into their houses from the dark. Until..."

"Go on," I said, pulling a pillow up around my legs for comfort.

"I had only left the house to find my brother. He was supposed to be home for dinner and with the night drawing in, my parents were worried about him. They didn't want me to go out either, but I promised I would find him and bring him home, I disobeyed them, leaving the house by the back door, not even time to leave a note. The wind was brisk outside as I pulled my jacket up around the collar, the clouds were swirling around the moon, drawing in an inky blackness as the world began to sink into quiet for the evening.

I had been walking for some time, about an hour, covering each end of the housing estate that we live on, walking as far as the town centre and even stopping to ask strangers if they had seen him on their travels. I was becoming weary, weary and afraid of what might happen to me if I returned home without him. I had hope that he would have returned home of his own accord, that I would walk through the front door to find him sat at the dining table, eating his roast, oblivious to the panic that he had caused. I decided to check the estate once more, though the strangest feeling of tiredness washed over me.

All at once my legs began to sink to the ground, they felt like lead weights dragging my body towards the ground. I was overcome with the need to rest and as I looked around, the darkness grew darker still and there was a thin mist, a fog, rising along the streets. The silence on the street had grown quieter still, somehow and all that I could hear was the sound of footsteps, long and dragging, getting closer still.

I pulled myself to standing, my legs still weighted and aching under the strain, I tried to walk away from the heavy dragging sound, but found I could no more walk than totter, as my legs felt as if they were about to give way. The footsteps grew closer still on the breeze and I heard the sound of a cough, a splutter as I saw the faint form of a figure come into view. My heart was racing now as I had no time to escape, no way of running as my legs would fail me. I sank to my knees, desperate and terrified.

I knew from the hulking shape and the dragging feet that Reginald had come to claim his next soul, I could barely hear him getting closer as my heart pounded in my chest, vibrating through my body. Slowly, as I felt his shadow loom above me, I began to turn my head to face the long-dead creature, the stuff of nightmares and empty threats before bed time. Towering above me was the old man that most thought to be nothing more than a legend. His crooked nose sneered down upon me under a huge black brimmed hat. His clothes, mismatched and worn looked nothing more than matted layers of grey under a deep brown overcoat which was singed and torn at the edges. But the thing I was drawn to most was his burlap sack, slung across his shoulder, a strange light, almost green in colour emanated from its fold and I could hear the distant sound of screaming, as if there were a thousand tortured souls trapped inside the material.

I could not look Reginald directly in the eye, I was frozen to the spot trying to drown out the hideous sounds muffled inside his mysterious bag and yet, with the click of one bony finger, the nail so long it had curled around the end, I was lifted from the floor, my legs levitated, my toes were scraping against the floor as his terrifying smile greeted me. I felt his chest rumble, like thunder, as he mouthed my name 'SCOTT' and with barely a sound he wrapped his fingers around my bony wrist and took a deep breath.

The rest was a blur, I could feel the very life force being sucked from me as the creature breathed inwards, taking parts of me with him. It was as if each memory, each tiny moment that made up my short life was being broken and extracted, like a jigsaw. I could feel pieces of me being carried on the wind, I felt as if I was shrivelling up. And yet, I did not scream, not that I could remember, I winced and stared into the face of the demon but still, despite all that I was losing to him, I would not give him a scream, I would not become another soul lost in his bag, in the universe that he slung across his shoulder. This seemed to anger him as he pulled another breath and sucked harder, his face pressing closer to me. My mind was weakening against him, each memory now fuzzy, the edges blurred as he realised he could hold me no longer. I felt myself slump against the floor as his skeletal fingers snapped again. I must have hit my head on the floor as I barely remembered the creature, skulking off dragging his feet behind him, nothing but the muffled sounds of trapped screams, of lost souls as he made his way onwards."

And that was how the boy had come to be hunched on my garden wall, that night. He had fought the horrifying presence of Reginald and had come face to face with his darkest fears. I thought the boy incredibly brave as he spoke, still ageing before my eyes. He had refused to give in to the Rasper's desire to feed on his fear, though in turn, he stole his lifeforce. Telling his story had almost used up the boy's energy as he crouched forward to grab another gulp of water. His voice had slowed, now croaking as if his breath was drawing short. His hair was the colour of chalk, the lines on his face were so deep he had become barely unrecognisable. And yet, I was unafraid of Scott, I knew his time here was growing shorter by the minute, I resolved to grab a blanket and place it over him as his eyes grew weary from the evening, the lifeforce ebbing from him ever more quickly. I turned my face away to grab a sofa blanket that usually lay folded on the floor. But when I turned back, Scott had become nothing more than an outline, like the beginnings of a drawing, a masterpiece, yet it signalled his end. I rushed to his side, his wide eyes piercing into me as he drew a last breath and faded into nothing more than dust particles that looked like they may have housed the shape of a boy, once upon a time.

***

My mum found me huddled against the chair the following morning, I must have drifted off to sleep, my head resting on the cushion of the armchair, where Scott's knees would have been. I touched my face at the tender memory of him, as he faded from my view. I sat up and looked at the empty chair, there was not a single trace of the boy who had sat there and relayed his terrifying tale, not a scrap of dust.

Though a part of me craved those silent evenings in the pitch black, pacing the garden and waiting for something beyond belief, something magical, I also knew that I had wanted it too much and that my curiosity had ultimately meant the death of my secret midnight jaunts. I had often closed my eyes and re-imagined the boy as he dissipated into fragments in front of my very eyes. I had often heard his tale whispered on the wind as I tried to settle my mind to bed at night. My mind would produce dreamlike tales of Reginald Rasper as he wandered through the back alley which connected our houses, seeking revenge on the poor lost father who burned his home to the ground. His crooked teeth would repeat the names of lost souls whom he had come to claim, his burlap bag growing heavy with the screams and cries of those he had captured. And though I grew older and moved away from the family home, the echoes of the lost boy's terrifying tale have stayed with me through the years. Needless to say, I left the house at night no longer, frightened of who would be waiting for me, next time.

I suppose that is why I am afraid of the dark, it no longer holds the magic and mystery I dreamed of as a young girl. It holds the torment that I recall from the boy's eyes, as he sat and told me of the crooked man who sucked his soul from the very depths of his body, it builds a cover from the nightmarish creatures of memory and imagination, the fingers that slip through the veil of life and death and pull at us. I suppose I am waiting for Reginald, listening for his footsteps, looking for his silhouette as it crouches on my wall. I am waiting for him to speak my name, for his fingers to curl around my wrists as he tries to wrestle my soul from my body, another one for his collection, another scream locked away in his bag of souls. And though I lock my doors and pull my covers up to my chin, I can hear footsteps, somewhere. I know he is real and that one day, he will win.

THE DOLLHOUSE AND HER

The shopkeeper looked at me and then back at the item I had just stood on his cash desk, his eyes lit up as he inspected the item in all its detail, miniaturised but perfect, a collectible to someone who was that way inclined. The sun was shining through the huge bay windows of the shop which was in every way the traditional layout one might imagine an antiques shop to be, as if it had jumped off the pages of a well-loved novel.

"How did you happen to have this is in your possession, if you don't mind my asking, Miss?" The shopkeeper was as polite as he was quiet.

"Please, call me Laura," I replied, smiling yet eager to retreat from the shop at the earliest opportunity. "It was given to me by my parents, I think my mother found it at a market, somewhere."

"And you don't have any reason to hang on to it?" The shopkeeper replied, glancing down at the expanse of my belly, swollen and brimming with new life.

"We don't have the room, sadly." I caught his gaze, rubbing my pregnant stomach as I felt a familiar kick from my tiny inhabitant.

The conversation carried on for a further ten minutes until I managed to break away from the friendly shopkeeper and his probing questions. I had left on a promise to call back in a few days, once the shopkeeper had had a chance to examine the item properly, to determine its worth. I left my name and phone number and went on my way, with several errands to run before the day was through.

Let that be the last of it, I thought to myself as I shut my car door and drove away, leaving the beautiful doll's house behind.

***

I was in the midst of a dreamless sleep when the buzz of the telephone on the bedside table startled me back to reality. I fumbled around for the light switch by my bed, hearing the contents of the table as they clattered to the floor. I picked up the receiver and whispered, though there was nobody else to disturb.

"Laura?" A disembodied voice called out.

"Speaking, who is this please?" Conscious that the hour was late and I was home alone, I felt waves of panic that the voice was not one that I recognised.

"Please forgive me," the voice replied. A man's voice, he was softly spoken and yet I could hear a sense of urgency in his voice. "This is Richard Carr, of Carr's Antiques Dealers."

"Mr Carr?" I lurched downwards to retrieve my watch that had fallen off the side of the table in the cascade, blinking, I turned it over in my hands. "It's almost midnight, whatever are you calling for at this time?"

"I'm so sorry it's so late," the urgency in Mr Carr's voice was increasing. "It's this doll's house that you brought to me, I didn't know who else to call."

"Calm down Mr Carr," I replied, trying to soothe his anxiety, though I fully understood. "Can you tell me what has happened?"

There was silence at the end of the phone for a few seconds and I thought I could hear the faint sound of crackling in the background, the remnants of burning embers.

"I think it is cursed." Mr Carr responded, the shake on his voice now unmistakeable.

I assured him that the house was not cursed and that perhaps there was some sort of fault with it, but he was persistent in his anxiety, without making any attempt to explain. I suppose he thought I knew. And the guilty part of me that had dropped the doll's house off at his antiques shop, knowing well what kind of havoc it could wreak to anyone who came into its possession, agreed to drive over to his shop and help if I could. Because I did know. The doll house was cursed.

When I arrived at the shop, the front door had been left ajar, as if someone had entered and had forgotten to close it behind them. I had parked my car further down the road, feeling anxious about being out alone at this time of night, a fear of the unknown pulsed through me as I walked towards the shop.

"Hello?" I called out, tapping lightly at the wooden exterior. "Mr Carr, are you in here?"

I heard nothing, the eerie silence of the street was almost deafening, even the street lights seemed dimmer, somehow. I pushed the door open, it creaked as it swung on its hinges, and started tentatively walking in.

By night, the shop looked like a menagerie of weird, abandoned goods, destined for a life of dust and neglect. I tripped over two small stools, presumably meant for children, which lay across the path way, whilst ducking under draped scarves and curtains that had been hanging for what seemed like decades. The usual inviting smell of the shop was now tinged with something musty, perhaps mould, it was like venturing into an undiscovered attic of broken treasures.

"Laura?" I heard Mr Carr call from somewhere at the back of the shop. "Is that you?"

A light appeared at the back of the shop, behind the till area, as if someone had opened a door, I could make out the shape of Mr Carr as he appeared in the archway, fumbling for a light switch. All at once, the shop was illuminated by the store lights, the chaos of the bric a brac, piled up in a precarious fashion was now fully lit and seemed less mysterious.

"I knocked," I said, making my across to the counter. "The door was open when I arrived, did you leave it open?"

"Come with me," he said hurrying me around the counter and through to the back of the shop. "I want to show you."

I followed Mr Carr through the makeshift archway that led to the back of his store. The archway had been crudely cut at a sloping angle and Mr Carr had to duck as he passed under, whilst dodging cardboard boxes which were spilling over with papers and packaged up stock. I followed Mr Carr through an alley and through another door, into what looked like a small version of a warehouse. The back of the shop was just as much a treasure trove as the front, boxes upon boxes were piled high against the walls, some were slumped and broken under the weight of the treasures they carried inside. There had been a little effort put in to decorate, an old Chat Noir poster, now rumpled and aged at the edges, was plastered on one wall with yellow Sellotape and there were some frames images dotted around the room. It felt surprisingly warm in the room, considering the walls were little more than treated concrete and there was no carpet.

Mr Carr had walked over to a small kitchenette area at the back of the warehouse, though the room itself was probably little more than six metres in length, he was pacing from one foot to the other, as he held a plastic kettle up at me with raised eyebrows.

"Yes, tea please," I said, eager to wake myself up. My bump moved around, the pressure shifted from one side of my rib cage to the other, as if it too was not impressed at the late-night awakening.

I heard the faint sound of the kettle as it started to rumble and boil on its stand, whilst Mr Carr busied himself finding and filling mugs. I became aware of the crackling sound again, the sound that I had strained to hear during Mr Carr's unexpected phone call. All at once, my eyes were drawn to the far end of the room and a slithering trail of smoke that crept up from behind what looked like a low pile of wooden storage trunks. Carefully, I began to walk over to it.

"Laura," Mr Carr shouted, he had noticed my sudden shift. "Please."

"Is that where the house is?" I quickened my pace, as Mr Carr hurried out from the kitchenette, leaving the kettle to scream to itself.

"Let me show you." He caught up with me, his stride quickened as he tried to stop me from pulling back the trunks.

He reached towards the trunks, but my movements were quicker, having almost twenty years on the man, I pushed the top trunk aside and gasped at the sight.

"I'm sorry," he cried softly, whilst resting his hand on my wrist. "I tried to stop it."

"I understand." I replied, though my face did not move from the scene.

The doll house, or what was left of it, was nothing but a blackened shell of the beautiful work of art that it had once been. The three-storey beauty, was now crippled to a blackened and hollow skeleton, burning under bright embers and taking every miniature piece of furniture and character with it. I spied the melted wax of what used to be one of the dolls, now sat forever in a scarred metal rocking chair, it was the most horrendous sight to behold, yet I felt relieved.

"Ever since you brought this house to me," Mr Carr began to explain, "I have been kept awake at night by such inexplicable sounds of crying children, people speaking in low tones, the faint crackling of fire. I thought I was going mad."

"Did you keep the house here, Mr Carr?" I replied, I was compelled to go and inspect the wreck of the house, but something about the gruesome, charred remains of the toy kept me away.

"Not at first," said Mr Carr, as he released his grip of my wrist. "I took the house to my flat, above the shop, so that I could inspect it a little more. I was going to do some research, some of the furniture pieces seemed incredibly old and worth quite a lot of money. Believe me, Laura, I had no intention of ripping you off."

"It's ok," I said, to reassure him. "That's why I brought it to you in the first place. I knew you would be able to get the best price for me and I, in turn, would be rid of the thing."

"You know, don't you?" Mr Carr looked at me, he had such kind eyes that I felt almost guilty for lumbering him with such a terrible thing, for a moment.

"Not exactly," I replied. "Only that I knew I needed to get that house and whatever was trapped inside it away from me and my baby."

We stayed silent for a moment longer, entranced by the embers of the dying fire as they danced around the crumbling walls of the doll's house. Mr Carr made his way back to the kitchenette, remembering the boiled kettle and the promise of tea and a few minutes later, I followed him. There was an old wooden table and two matching chairs that were placed in the centre of the kitchen area, he gestured for me to take a seat, as he brought a plate of biscuits and placed them on the table.

"Did you set fire to it?" I asked Mr Carr, as he took his own place on the chair opposite me.

"I honestly don't know," he replied, as he pulled the chair in closer to the table, being careful not to wobble the drinks as he did so. "It's all a blur, there were terrible sounds coming from it, I had thought about it but, I don't remember whether I struck the match, or the match was struck for me."

We sat in silence again, I felt tiredness creeping in as my eyes grew heavy, I picked my mug of tea up and wrapped my hands around it for comfort.

"Why did you ask me here?" I queried, watching Mr Carr as his gaze fell upon the smoke from the fire again.

He looked pensive, for a moment, as he sat back in his chair and picked up his own mug.

"I've been in this business for thirty-five years, Laura," he began. "It's not always easy to source the right kind of things for the shop, or for your customers. Everything I work with has some sort of story, you get to understand how things feel when you hold them in your hands for the first time. Some give a great warmth, as soon as you touch them, as if they have been loved for centuries. Others can be cold, almost hard to touch, and those are the things that often do not pass my front door. I cannot sell something that doesn't have love imprinted in it."

I put my mug down and sat forward in anticipation of his story, I was both fascinated and frightened.

"In all my thirty-five years as an antiques dealer," he continued. "In fact, forty, if you include my apprentice work, I have never come across such an exquisite piece of work that seems to have so much…evil inside it. I've always considered myself a rational man, one that buys and sells pieces based on his best judgement, of course, but not someone who genuinely believes that items and things can be…haunted."

"Go on." I said, as Mr Carr's face dropped in a state of confusion.

"I think you are a rational woman, Laura," he continued. "I picked that up from you the very day you brought this thing to me. You are not someone who is easily scared, nor are you someone who believes in fairy tales and yet, I know you had these experiences too.

When things became worse, I moved the house downstairs and I thought of nothing other than calling you for help, for advice. But now you are here, now that we both know that this house contains something…not right. I want to hear your story, I want you to tell me everything."

Mr Carr's eyes widened, the glare of the copper light above him shone through his deep green irises. He was a troubled man, the weight of the past few days since my first encounter with him had taken their toll, much as they had taken their toll on me.

I sat for a moment, watching as what remained of the doll house crumbled in on itself, the beautiful décor now etched with black and scorched orange, faded into nothing. I smoothed the lines of my ill-fitting dress, responding to a kick from my bump; I felt nervous but compelled to tell my story. Slowly, I began.

"It all began about four months into my pregnancy, which had been unexpected and difficult. David and I had been together for about three years when we found out we were expecting a baby, a beacon in what had become a tired and dull relationship. Although those first few weeks felt surreal, the yearning of motherhood had become second nature to me almost instantly, for David it would take a lot longer. But, we had moved in together, both of our jobs were stable and we were content, to the point of insanity.

My parents had taken the news well, though they too were shocked, at first. They had promised to give their utmost support from that point onwards, though I always suspected that they had doubts about my relationship with David and whether he was the right man for me. Like all parents, they had conjured up a fairy tale romance for their only daughter, with someone who would sweep me off my feet, someone who I would be able to depend and rely on. David and I were thrown together through mutual friends and, despite my uncertainty about him from our first date, I had continued to see him, each time we met, my fondness of his awkward sense of humour and the way that my skin would light up when he touched me had grown until the relationship had bloomed on unstable soil. In truth, I had fallen in love with the very things that could not keep a relationship alive, but I was not prepared to admit or accept it.

My mother paid me a surprise visit a few weeks after we had told them the news, I had been busy sorting through our spare attic room, hopeful that we could turn it into a guest bedroom, so that the small room on the first floor as a nursery for the new arrival. The first hints of spring were hanging in the air that day and the intricate frost patterns that adorned the skylight windows were long melted, making way for bluer skies and warmer breezes that fluttered against the skin.

David had taken himself out cycling for the day, needing to destress from work and, I suspect, his unwillingness to be involved with the excitement surrounding the new baby. I had been told that such happy and surreal times would put strain on the strongest relationships and, whilst I had busied myself with preparations for the arrival, who had already begun to fill his or her space in my heart, I pushed aside the feelings of neglect that I had felt emanating from David. The precarious strings of our relationship had long been loosening their threads, I feared.

Mother had already made herself at home by the time I had brewed a fresh pot of tea; her coat had been carelessly slung over the back of the sofa and her small suitcase, that was still fit to bursting, had been placed on the bottom step of the staircase, as if it were expecting to be taken to the spare room imminently. What struck me most, as I entered my lounge with a tray of tea and cake, was the large object that had been placed on the coffee table in my absence, whilst mother sat on the sofa, eagerly anticipating my opinion on it.

"I couldn't resist." she said, her face beaming as she took the coffee cup from my tray and looked at me, expectantly.

"Mum," I replied, whilst I precariously placed the tray on the coffee table's edge, careful not to scratch the neat paintwork of the beautiful doll's house. "It's beautiful, but we don't know what we are even having, yet."

"Oh, rubbish," she said, lurching forward for a biscuit from the tray. "Any child will get a small piece of joy from playing with something this beautiful."

I smiled as I took up a place in the armchair opposite her, something about my otherwise logical and independent mother had softened since she had heard the news of the pregnancy. I had always seen so much of her in myself, as if she had formed and moulded me in her own image. I held her gaze for a little while, as she sipped on the hot tea that was still steaming in the cup, she looked a little more fragile.

"Take a look inside," she said, gesturing towards the doll's house. "I don't know why, it reminded me of the house we used to live in when you were little. Perhaps you don't remember."

"Vaguely," I said, pensive, as I put my cup down and reached across to take a closer look at the house. My bump was growing by the day now, or at least that was how it felt, I still misjudged how far my torso could travel before it hit the alien being that was nestling inside me. "We moved when I was about six though, didn't we?"

"We did." mother replied, after another short burst of silence. I watched as her brow furrowed and she shook her head, as if in disagreement with something she had said to herself.

The house itself was indeed a beautiful work of art, I could not remember seeing something so intricate, as I admired the detailing of the painted brick work and the vines that cascaded down along the wall. The roof was tiled with individual pieces and there was even a tiny crow that sat on top of the chimney. The windows were framed in a glossy white and each set had a different coloured pair of fabric curtains framing the inside of the miniature rooms. I bent down further still, as far as my bump would allow me and took in the marvellous detailing of the bronze door knocker and letterbox that stood proudly against the bright red door, which also held a tiny red and green holly and berry wreath as if in preparation for Christmas.

I pushed the miniature door open with my little finger and peered inside through the hallway. I could see a tiny pair of boots that had been nailed into place by the brushed welcome mat and what felt like little coat hooks that had been placed along the back of the door. I wiggled my finger in further, ignoring instructions from my mother to open the house up by its latches, to try and feel and see the house from the eyes of a tiny person, mesmerised by the details that had been added by such a talented artist. I snapped my hand back almost immediately as I felt something small bite the very tip of my finger.

"Are you alright?" Mother exclaimed, as I pulled my finger to my mouth and winced in pain.

"Something just...bit me." I said, examining my finger for any kind of mark. I felt stupid, ridiculous for pulling away from the house, but the pain was quick and sharp and completely unexpected.

"Perhaps there is a loose nail or something in the floorboards?" Mother replied, as she leaned forward to open the latch on the house and inspect further.

"Yes, perhaps." I said, holding my finger close to me and ignoring the swelling and the two tiny sets of teeth marks that were visible on the tip.

***

Mother had scoured the floorboards of the doll's house for the remainder of that afternoon, whilst pulling out tiny pieces of perfectly recreated furniture and four members of a doll family that 'lived' in the house. There was a 'Mother', a 'Father', and two younger children. Rather absurdly, there was a nursery room in the attic space too, but no baby doll to fill it; presumably it had been lost somewhere down the line. I had lost interest in the house after the strange incident, though I had convinced myself that the mark must have been nothing more than a nick from a loose nail or something sharp that needed repairing. I busied myself with taking mother's suitcase upstairs and helping her to unpack, we talked through plans for the new nursery room and how I wanted to decorate the attic room before the baby arrived, if I could find the time and energy. I thought nothing more about the dollhouse until David returned home just before dinner and questioned it as it was still sat in its same place on the coffee table.

"Do we even have room for something like that?" He said, ungrateful and with a hint of sarcasm in his voice; he forever accused my parents of pandering to buying large gifts and using money as a way to secure affection from me. "It's not even like it's going to play with something like that for years."

"Perhaps not," I replied, my voice stern as I chopped salad in the kitchen area, eyeing him as he muttered something under his breath. "But it was a very nice gesture and it would not hurt you to be appreciative towards my mother."

David didn't respond, he had sat down to rest his legs from a long afternoon of cycling. His earlier use of the word 'IT' for our child bore into my ears. To him, it may have been nothing more than a fickle choice of words and a clear indication that he had no preference over the gender; to me it screamed his indifference, it screamed that we were at different phases of life; whilst I was becoming more accustomed to nestling into the idea of a cosy home life and the birth of a real family, he was moving farther away from it.

Dinner was quiet, but pleasant, as my mother talked to David about his cycling trips and the surrounding areas. I was grateful for her direct and unstoppable nature throughout dinner, it drowned out the uncomfortable truths that were knocking at the door, threatening to make themselves known, to become louder and louder until I could ignore them no longer.

David and I went up to bed shortly after my mother did, though it felt earlier than it actually was. We had whiled away the evening with a new television programme on the BBC, something that David had been desperate to watch and had received good reviews in the newspapers. I sat on the edge of the bed, adjusting myself to the nightly activity of my bump, as it tended to come alive as I laid down for at least the first two hours. I struggled into a non-maternity nightdress and clambered into bed, under the fluffy covers, my head hit the pillows and relaxed against them almost instantly. I felt myself falling into that strange place, somewhere between a deep sleep and an awareness of the real world, as I heard David switch off the bathroom light and return to the bedroom without uttering a word. I rubbed my belly, almost subconsciously as I gave in to the rhythm of my very active baby and cradled it from outside its fleshy boundaries, whilst I soothed us both to a calm sleep. And I told myself it was just my imagination, seeping from this world into the world of dreams, as I heard the faint crying of a small child, as if it were waiting outside my bedroom door, waiting for me to wake up and speak to it.

***

At first I said nothing about the noise I thought I had heard, I chose to dismiss it, much like the strange bite mark, whose ethereal teeth marks were still vaguely visible when I awoke the following day. I put it down to tiredness, to the consistent feeling of anxiousness as I tiptoed around my partner and he, in turn, tiptoed around me. I had taken a few days of annual leave in order to keep my mother company and Monday seemed like the perfect day to make a big breakfast and tackle some of the items we had yet to buy for the new arrival.

Mother was already dressed and brewing the kettle when I appeared downstairs, I had briefly glanced at the clock when I had woken up and, although it wasn't late, I was grateful to not have to be a slave to my alarm clock for a few days.

"I found some bread in the freezer," mother chirruped as she poured fresh, steaming tea into two large mugs. "I presume you can still have this stuff, it's decaffeinated?"

"Yes," I replied, taking a seat at the kitchen table, though my eyes wandered over to the dollhouse, which was still sat on the coffee table, pristine and inviting. "Just one though."

"David was up early this morning, he's gone to work already," mother remarked as she reached for the fridge door, she had already made herself at home and I was becoming so used to her being here. "He said something about the neighbours keeping him up all night."

"Really?" I queried. "I didn't hear a thing."

"No," mother replied. "I didn't hear anything either, it was really quite strange. You know I'm fond of David, but he seems very...at odds with himself at the moment, Laura."

I wanted to talk to her, at that moment, whilst the two of us sipped morning tea and brooded on life together, I had never felt closer to her.

A swell of something, almost nauseous, that I had kept for so long, hidden under blankets of self-doubt and was rising. Yet, I felt I could not let it go; the whispers and the promise of something bigger and louder were banging inside my head but the idea that I would let mother down if I told her was bigger still. So I took a deep breath and reached for the mug that she passed me, I smiled sweetly and pushed the anxiety about David and our relationship to deep crevices of my mind, hoping to shut them away for at least the remainder of her stay.

"Do you know your neighbours, Laura?" Mother asked, as I got up to help with breakfast preparations, my bump kicked against the side of my swollen belly as I rubbed it.

"A little," I said. "We've spoken a few times, they seem very friendly."

"That's great," said mother. "Perhaps the children might even grow up to be friends? David said their baby can't be very old, must be only one year or two."

I stopped in my tracks, remembering the faint sound of crying as it cascaded through the bedroom walls as I tried to get to sleep the night before, the very sounds that I thought had invaded only my mind, conceived by my own imagination.

"They don't have children." I said, before I made a swift exit to the bathroom, feeling the rise of bile and nausea and perhaps the remnants of words that I should have said long ago.

***

They have no children.

This statement played over in my mind as I finished the breakfast dishes and feigned some interest in my mother's plans for the day. I had felt a shudder as I muttered those words to mother, conscious that it meant that the soft, almost inaudible cry I thought I had heard at the bedroom door, had perhaps not been a figment of my imagination. I felt a sharp prod in my back, as I faced the window, like the point of a fingernail stabbing me in the back, it shook me from my thoughtful state, as I turned around to find the culprit.

There was nobody in the room, even my mother had disappeared, presumably to another room. Though it occurred to me that I didn't consider that she might have done it, she could be stern at times, but never violent. Whilst I didn't expect to see the familiar face of my mother standing behind me, it did occur to me that I didn't quite know how or what I was expecting to find. The room was silent, there was not a thing out of place, not even the chill breeze of someone exiting the room, swishing the door behind them. My heart raced as I listened out for footsteps, but there was nothing.

My attention was drawn to the doll's house, which I had not opened since the incident the day before. And whilst the logical side of my brain could find no reason for this, I felt a force stronger than logic place an unknown blame on the house, for the strange occurrences that had weaved their way through the house, subtle and impossible to ignore. All the while the pain in my back spread through me, a sensation almost like burning, coursed along my veins and I winced at the pain. It was impossible to ignore.

I walked over to the house as it was sat in the stillness of the lounge, the quaint and beautiful features were so precise and so beautifully drawn and painted, it was as though it had been shrunken, miniaturised from a real-life scene. I nodded to myself as I dismissed the thought and carefully lifted the sprung latch and opened the house up, my fingers were shaking as I pulled the two wooden blocks of the house apart. I was greeted with a mock scene that my mother had obviously been putting together the day before. The 'mother' doll was stood in the kitchen, whilst one child stood behind her, their soft fabric bellies were leaning against chairs and worktops to keep them in an upright position. The other child doll appeared to be asleep in an upstairs bedroom, with a soft floral quilt covering most of its face and body, and the attic nursery was still desolate and quiet, without a baby doll to fill it. What unnerved me most was the 'father' doll, which was slumped face down on the sofa in the lounge room, I'm not sure what compelled me to pick it up and replace it to a sitting position but as I did so, I dropped the doll in sheer fright. For where an ageing face with painted features had once been, there was now nothing but two black etched lines across his face, scored as if he had been tortured with a match.

***

"I just think you're overreacting," mother's voice was calm and collected, as I held the deformed doll in my hand, my fingers scraping along the etched cross on his face.

"Mother," I stopped her in her tracks, exasperated at her willingness to overlook such a frightening thing, which had echoed my own behaviour since the appearance of the doll's house. "I'm not sure about this house. Ever since you brought it in - and I really don't want to sound ungrateful – there have been strange things happening. I can't put my finger on it, I just don't know if I want the house."

"Nonsense," Mother replied in a shrill voice. "One too many ghost stories, that's the problem there."

"No," I replied, cutting her off in the middle of her dismissal. "Firstly, I have tiny teeth marks on my hand, then both David and I are kept awake by the crying of a child who doesn't seem to exist and now the etching on the doll."

I left out the part about the scratch to her. But on close inspection in my walled bedroom mirrors, I did appear to have a deep red welt, about the size of a small ruler, that had been scored into my back. I knew I made no sense as I spoke, I barely made sense to myself, but my instinct had long overtaken logic and I just knew, somehow, that the house carried something evil with it. Something potentially dangerous.

David agreed with my mother, of course. Opting to get involved as little as he could for the sake of saving us all from an argument. By the time we went to bed that evening, mother had decided to cut her stay short to just one more day, for fear of 'upsetting me further', whilst David trudged up to bed without so much as a goodnight to anyone.

The dreams that came that night were the strangest. I could not see people or places as much as sense burning and fire, I felt as though I were trapped with nothing but clouds of smoke surrounding me, everything was black and foggy and glowing embers lit the way in an unfamiliar dreamscape. My baby tossed and turned in rhythm to my movements as I fought my subconscious, desperate to know more but seeing only black and fire and hearing the faintest murmurs to suggest that there were other people who were trapped with me, if indeed we were trapped at all.

The faint sound of crying woke me up, it sounded soft and distant and yet loud enough to be outside my bedroom door again. I fumbled for the light switch, shaken from the horrible feeling hanging over me from the dream and the atmosphere that had shaken my home over the past few days. As I switched the light on, I could see my phone lit up and blinking digits at me – it was nearly 3.00 a.m. I felt for David to wake him up, but when I turned around he was not in bed. The bedroom door was shut tight, the only sign that he may have got out of bed might have been a door left ajar. I was struck by a sudden breeze whirling around my shoulders as I looked up at the curtain, which billowed in the wind. We had not had any windows open that evening, nor for that week for that matter; the days were becoming longer but the nights were still chilly and often damp.

I swung my legs over the bed and tiptoed across the close the window, the soft whimpering had ceased and the night was dead still. I pushed one curtain aside to pull the large window closed and, for just a moment, thought I saw the faint shadow of someone running across the front garden, away from the house. The figure looked tall but broad, a male figure that sprinted away from view almost as soon as they had come into view. I didn't know this at the time, but that was the last time I would see David. I struggle to remember anything of his disappearance, as I didn't even fathom that the male figure I thought I saw sprinting across and away from my garden might have been him. I do remember the hearing a deafening scream, a howl in the distance that made me jump back into bed and hide.

The events of my dreams and the hideous, mournful crying that had woken me again had unnerved me and so, putting all the landing lights on, I crept downstairs to make a drink. As I crept downstairs, I could hear a crackling sound, faint at first but getting louder as if it were gathering power and force. It was surreal and yet familiar, as I was met in my lounge by the same cloud of smoke that had invaded my dream. I fought against the clouds of smoke, shots of bright orange burning embers seemed to fall towards me, though I could not feel them touch me. I felt as though I was in a bubble and though I tried to scream for help, I could not hear my own voice above the thundering sounds of the fire around me.

I thought of my baby, of inhaling the fumes from the fire and I dropped to the floor, as low as I could, to crawl across to the kitchen, to the back door, where I could escape. I could reach for nothing to cover my mouth and nose with, so I stuck my face as far inside my dressing gown as I could, to block out the fumes and the returning sound of the disembodied crying. I struggled towards the back door, keeping my eyes closed and not wanting to see any of the happenings around me. I thought of my mother, sleeping peacefully upstairs and how much I wanted to go to her and drag her out with me; but the fire was strong and its heat permeated through my clothes, I could feel myself melting and I knew I had one chance to save my baby.

I crawled through the house, my knees were red raw as they rubbed against the tile floor of the kitchen, scraped along the grouting as at last I felt my way towards the silver metal of the back door. I fumbled along the rim of the door to find the keyhole and grabbed the keyring when I felt the familiar metal clasp in my hand, I twisted it with what little energy I had remaining and felt myself leap forward at the chill night air, as the door swung back on its hinges. I had pulled myself to safety, my hands had felt the dew of the garden grass patch and its dampness was soothing. I collapsed onto my side, feeling along my pregnant belly for some sign that the baby was safe and I felt a heavy sigh of relief escape me as I was greeted with a large kick to the rib cage. Exhausted, I fell into a deep and dreamless sleep.

***

I blinked in the early morning sun as it rose in the sky, unaware of where I was at first, I wiped the dewy blades of grass that were digging into my face and turned to sit up. Memories came flooding back to me, layer upon layer of strange images and the running figure and the terrible fire. I caught my breath as I sat up to face the house and found my mother, sitting on the garden bench opposite, a cup of tea in her hand and a concerned and worried look shadowing her face.

Together, my mother and I entered the house again to find everything still intact. Each room, each piece of furniture, each precious thing that made this my home, everything remained unchanged. There was an eerie stillness about the place, that morning, as if it had been a silent witness to a horrible scene. I touched everything that I passed, my hands were still trembling with the events of the evening and there were still so many unanswered questions.

My mother and I sat together and talked about the strange happenings, I told her about my dream and how it had spilled over into the most real of realities as I had battled smoke and fire in my house. We examined my back and the scarring on my little finger, where the tiniest teeth marks were still visible and when David's work called the house phone, its shrill noise both uninvited and unwanted, I feared the worst but could fathom no explanation. I was lost without the uncertainty that David had brought to the relationships, I missed missing him.

And on that morning, when I had had a chance to clear the debris of my mind and grieve for the simple life that had existed before these inexplicable events had occurred, I opened up the doll's house one last time, not knowing what to expect other than gruesome images created from fear; I was unsurprised to find the 'father' doll had vanished. He had disintegrated into thin air, leaving behind a tiny bundle that had now been placed in the top attic nursery. I picked up the tiny bundle, wrapped in a strange cotton cloth; a baby doll, swaddled and sleeping peacefully. Except for its face, a face that had the same etchings scored across its face as the 'father' doll had had. Its featureless face looked contorted under the deep 'X', so much so that I threw it back in the cot and closed the doors on the house for the last time.

Mother stayed a while longer, we slept downstairs together for a few days whilst we waited to hear of any news of David, to no avail. And the house was brought to you the very next day."

Mr Carr's eyes had glazed over a little, as I finished the last of my tale and in doing so, placed my empty mug back on the table. The chink of the china as it hit the wood brought him back to life.

"Fascinating." was the only word he could conjure, several times, before he straightened himself up in his chair and regained awareness of the space he was in again.

"It was long," I tried to make light of my story. "Sorry, I didn't mean to keep you."

"I needed to hear it, Laura," he added my name as an afterthought. "I'm so sorry for what has happened to you."

"It's not your fault," I said, my attention was drawn over to the far corner and the smouldering wreck of the house again. "I'm not sure if or how I will ever make peace with it all. I only know that I needed to be rid of the thing."

"Have they found him?" Mr Carr's words cut through mine, as if hurrying them would make them less brutal, somehow. "Your partner, are they still looking?"

"They're still looking," I looked back down at my lap, conscious of how crazy my story must have sounded, but thankful that Mr Carr had been so accepting of it. "They think he might have fallen in the river, might have been carried away by the tide, it's a strong current down there."

"I'm so sorry for your loss, Laura," he gestured a kind hand towards me, we had become kindred spirits in the wake of something so strange and terrifying. "If indeed he is lost to you."

"Thank you." For the first time since David's disappearance, I allowed the tears to escape, I felt their hot, burning wetness as they fell down each cheek, a drip at first, then a silent stream, and I felt nothing but relief. I felt like a bottle that had been corked for too long; the cork, though buoyant, held fast, clawing at logical explanation after logical explanation. Though the trauma had cracked something deep below the surface, each and every strange and inexplicable moment that had occurred since that dreaded house had entered my life, had chipped away at it. The police were still looking, though my heart had sunk long ago at the thought that David would actually return.

We said nothing more to each other, Mr Carr and I. Not that night, nor after that as it happened. He could see that I was distressed and he didn't know how to comfort me, nor I to him that could ever atone for the curse that I had laid upon him when I discarded the doll's house at his shop. I dried my tears with the back of my woollen cardigan and made my excuses to leave. It didn't occur to me until the next day that Mr Carr had not uttered a word about his own experiences with house, only that he had listened to mine with such a sense of knowing, that I could only assume he had felt and seen the same thing. I only hoped that he didn't have a family that the strange being could play with, or harm. I supposed that I would never know.

I would often drive past the antique shop on my journeys to and from work and, later, when the baby was born, I would often take a stroll out to the town centre, hoping to catch a glimpse of Mr Carr without having to set foot inside the shop itself; the whole evening had become entangled in the mess and devastation of the doll's house and, much like a victim of trauma, I knew it would be years before I would be brave enough to step inside the confines of the shop again.

I did see him last week though as I was taking the baby out for a morning stroll, before the onset of forecast rain for the next two days was due to set in. The familiar sight of Mr Carr and his speckled pepperpot hair, his age-old uniform of a white shirt with deep green corduroy trousers, appeared in the doorway of his shop, amid silhouettes of spilling trunks and hanging trinkets. He seemed in his world, answering to nobody as he busied about his domain with a sense of fervour. He was just as I had always remembered him, before the incident, yet I was compelled to stop and watch him for just a second. I watched as he squeezed his way past the bric a brac that had been casually tossed on the floor of the window display, almost walking on tiptoes and carrying a large object that he had appeared to make space for. I gazed on, though keeping a safe distance, as he placed the object on a large wooden block, to set it apart from the other products in the window. I almost jumped out of my skin as Mr Carr shot around to face me directly from the window, as if he had sense someone staring at him. He had the same kindly face that I remembered, but there was something in his mannerisms that felt somewhat stark and awkward, strange, he stayed still and stared back at me for what seemed like hours, before lifting his hand up in a slow and steady waving motion. I was transfixed on him, I hardly noticed the baby as he wriggled himself awake and snuffled around at his surroundings. I lifted my hand and waved back at him, smiling though I still did not want to face my fears and enter the shop itself. Mr Carr began to remove himself from the window and, in his absence, I could see the new item as it sat proudly in his window display. Though I was stood at a safe distance from it, my heart started racing and rattling against my ribcage as I tried to make sense of what I was seeing, though I knew it would be impossible. For the same details that I had been in awe of all those months ago, were the same charred remains that I had witnessed at the back of Mr Carr's shop.

The house itself was indeed a beautiful work of art, I could not remember seeing something so intricate, as I admired the detailing of the painted brick work and the vines that cascaded down along the wall. The roof was tiled with individual pieces and there was even a tiny crow that sat on top of the chimney. The windows were framed in a glossy white and each set had a different coloured pair of fabric curtains framing the inside of the miniature rooms. The perfect, miniature bronze door knocker and letterbox still stood proudly against the bright red door, which also held a tiny red and green holly and berry wreath as if in preparation for Christmas. It was perfect, again.

A MOST TRANSPARENT
GENTLEMAN

"You found it." he said, as the door creaked shut behind me.

It was quiet, busier than I had imagined, but quiet still. A bar, a hovel of rickety bench chairs and tables, were scattered against the unnerving slope of a tumbledown ceiling, framing a short, stumpy wooden bar, placed just off the centre along the back wall. There was a man stood behind it, shuffling to the sounds of clinking glasses, the quiet roars of secret talk and laughter.

"Yes." I replied, shaking the droplets of rainfall from my coat, as the man gestured towards the free chair, opposite him. "I must admit, I had no idea this was here."

"I hope my directions were helpful." said the man, Mr Carter. "It is a well-kept secret, that's the beauty of a place like this."

"It's….quaint." I hesitated, looking around the room once more, studying the pictures on the walls, faded drawings of landscapes and town scenes, some so browned, cracked and weathered with age, they almost faded into the walls themselves.

"You're quite welcome." Mr Carter's eyes gestured across to the bar, his face never moving, not cracking once. I took this as an opportunity to order a drink, before the interview commenced.

I stood at the bar for a short time, careful to make little eye contact with the barman, or the other people, situated at the tables, there was discomfort in the air, something that tugged at the bottom of my skirt, that twisted in the loose curls of my hair. I felt out of place here, not used to my surroundings. I wanted to get the interview over with, as soon as I could, and get out of there. Whoever had heard of a bar like this? Hidden from the streams of bustling crowds in the city, the ghosts whose footsteps echoed above my head, as I drank in the stale atmosphere of the secret parlour. I had near enough fallen into the concealed entrance, had it not been for the gentleman, who had caught my arm as I slipped. I returned to my seat, a cool tumbler of gin in my hand, holding his gaze as the glass, dripping over ice, formed small pools in the creases of my hand.

Mr Carter sat, transfixed upon a spot by the front door; by a small window beside a cracked coat-hanging stand. His gaze was severe, his eyes glazed and widened in terror, I stopped short at the strange sight of a strange man, a stranger man than I had first, perhaps, judged.

"Are you alright, Mr Carter?" I said, not wishing to raise my voice.

"Quite, quite." he said, his body shuddering, his eyes darting back towards me as he regained himself. "I do apologise. A memory, I think."

"A memory of what?" Intrigued, I pressed him further.

"My dear girl," he relaxed a little, his back pressed against the wall, as he readjusted his balance on the hard, wooden bench. "I wouldn't expect you to understand, it's just, I don't imagine you believe in ghosts, do you?"

I thought for a while, conjuring an answer that most suited my undecided nature towards these things. I had always given bumps in the night and ghoulish tales such little of my time and interest, being at one with the solid world around me.

"I wouldn't say I didn't believe, Mr Carter," I began, "I can't say I have ever had an experience to raise my question of belief."

"They exist, Miss Savage, of that I am certain." Mr Carter leaned in closer. "They say he haunts this place, the street above us. The previous owner. I knew of him a little. A very proud man, handsome and tall, friendly and forgiving. He died, a tragic car accident, some years back. I had never really thought of him, until…"

"Until what, Mr Carter?" I pressed again.

"Until I saw his face appear in the window, just behind you." I jumped as his eyes darted behind me.

"Impossible!" I scoffed, ignoring the sense of fear in my stomach.

"It is my belief, Miss Savage, that logic cannot always provide a suitable explanation." His face dropped into a crooked smile. "Say, how did you manage to find this place, in the end?"

A swift subject change, I sat my drink down on the table and readjusted myself on the small stool. Settled and, for some reason, wary of others listening in on our conversation, I began to tell Mr Carter the story of the man who had pulled me after my fall in the busy street, the man who led me to the hidden front door, the gateway to this strange place.

"He was charming." I began my tale, save for the memory of the cold chill that blew from the gentleman's mouth as he spoke in my direction, as if winter itself was encased between his lips. "You see, Mr Carter, I make little habit of coming out to meet strangers of an evening, I do not get tangled with the crowds, it is these busy times I cannot abide, the hustle as everyone fights to get out of this cold, wet weather."

"Do go on, Miss Savage." Mr Carter's tone held a tinge of annoyance.

"I'm sorry." I replied, rubbing my hands along my dress as I did so, attempting a nervous laugh. "Well, I suppose, what I was trying to say, was that I felt lost. Lost and overwhelmed by the rain, the bundles of people making their own short, sharp ways home, by the directions you had been so kind to write down for me. I tripped on the hem of my dress. A piece of lace trim, that had been snagging for days, had caught under the heel of my boot, causing me to lurch forwards, against the stride of the crowds, almost losing my grip completely on the unfamiliar steps.

I had little time to catch my breath, before a gloved hand reached out to mine, pulling me to safety. I felt the soft hide of black leather, the momentary glide as he pulled me up, before I took any notice of him. The stranger. I fell close against his chest, my hands splaying into his woollen overcoat, my eyes darting to focus on this silhouette of his top hat, as I caught my breath. The world melted away from us, for just a moment, as my eyes fell upon his face. A most handsome face, his smile was crooked, revealing the faint lines of yellowing teeth as he loosened his grip on my hand.

I immediately apologised for my error, thanking him for his efforts, brushing my dress down, with nerves as I turned to walk away.

'You are lost.' the stranger said.

'No, no.' I replied as I turned around to face him. 'No, I'm…well…yes, I'm looking for The Cellar Door, I am meeting someone there.'

The stranger laughed, his smile widening across his face as his soft, gloved hand pointed towards the stone steps that I had almost tripped over. I followed the point of his slender, coated arm, the long fingers encased in his glove, he smiled at me, to himself, as he proffered his other hand to guide me down the stairs. He muttered as he led me down the steps, nothing that I could remember, sentences or questions, they could have been either. The last thing I remember, I turned to thank the man who had been so courteous to escort me to my secret destination, to find he had vanished, disappeared into the night. Leaving nothing but the feel of creeping strangeness, as I made my way into the secret parlour, to you."

"An interesting story, Miss Savage," Mr Carter sounded somewhere in between bemused and afraid, "but you seem to be troubled by this stranger?"

"Perhaps, Mr Carter." I replied, replaying the moment my strange gentleman vanished from sight. "Confused, more. I remember he was ice cold, darting out of nowhere to save me as I tripped, it seemed almost meant."

"Those that linger on your mind, linger on this earth, longer than they should, Miss Savage." Mr Carter was cryptic, which prompted me to check my watch, conscious that I had not even begun the interview yet.

"I don't think I follow you." I replied, flashing a half smile, as Mr Carter sat forward, his voice quietening.

"A most transparent gentleman, a handsome face, a kind and mysterious demeanour?" Mr Carter began. "Your character sounds familiar, Miss Savage. Tell me, has it occurred to you, through the course of this meeting that your man and my ghost were made of the same stuff?"

"The face you saw?" I replied, eyes widened in terror as my skin crawled at the memory of his wintry presence. 'The man who died in the accident?'

"Oh yes, Miss Savage." The wind blew around Mr Carter as another shadowy guest entered the building, slamming the door behind them. "I do believe you have met your first ghost, your first encounter with the Gentleman of Bridlesmith."

POPPY AND THE DEVIL

I cannot remember the first time my mother started talking to The Devil. She changed, stretched overnight, filled the gaps that had been missing. We were two, plus Cook and John, the gardener. Then we were living with an invisible entity. My mother welcomed Him in, fell in love all over again, it seemed, demanding that we set a place for Him at our dining table.

I didn't see Him at first, I didn't feel Him. I supposed He had crept in through the back door, left ajar during the hazy, close summer evenings that lay thundering over us as we fought for sleep and comfort. I supposed He had sidled past the scullery, the pantry door and the kitchen, obscured by the wafts of flour and cheerful chirping from Cook. He must have clicked up the little stone steps and along the hallway, the sun beaming down on Him, as He made His way to our dining room table, where my mother had served Him a plate of meat and vegetables, and nearly all the dumplings. He had not been here before, then suddenly He was here, filling the empty spaces with His nothingness, His blackness.

It started with muttering. Each step of the journey, He came to see my mother and took a little piece of her with Him, every time. I counted her beautiful, flailing ebony locks, tucked away, tight to her head, as they started to come loose. Pin by pin, strand by strand, she unravelled a little more. I would see my mother every day, I could see the little changes in her, I was losing her to the whims of an invisible guest. Cook said not to worry, that my mother was the victim of imagination; that He wasn't really there, skulking behind the curtains, announcing His place at our table, eating nearly *all* he dumplings and making my mother mutter things under her breath.

I cannot remember the first time my mother started talking to The Devil, but I never ate dumplings again.

* * *

My mother had never been one to mutter. When I think back to the time before, when there were three of us, plus Cook and John, and laughter used to fill the house, captured in echoes that ran from the huge oak front door to the garden conservatory, you could feel the warmth of my mother from her presence alone. She used to sway between thoughtful silence and smiles during dinner, unleashing her conversation when my father left the room. He was a quiet man, when he was here, it was funny how his absence seemed to seep from every pore of every room when he was gone. For years, I longed to hear my father's very special silence again, to be comforted by his steady breathing; strong, silent, but there.

But he left one day and he never returned. And my mother fell deaf to the world for a little while. I think that's what happens when you truly love someone and they can't stay with you, the rest of the world comes to a temporary halt, all else is drowned out by the dull thumping of your own broken heart. Some days she stayed in her bedroom, others she made an effort to get up, dressed and walk about the house, feeling every wall, every wooden beam, as if needing to be reassured that these most solid of possessions were still there. There were glimpses of her freedom, erratic waltzes by candlelight; I would catch her smiling at me over an evening meal from time to time, and I would hope that she could be fixed.

But that was then.

Now there was just me and her, and her muttering. And a new place set at the table. The three of us existing somewhere, between the oak front door and the garden conservatory, but worlds apart, and haunted by only ever the faintest of laughter. She muttered words I tried to ignore but could not fathom, numbers sometimes, held between her deep breaths like a secret language, between Him and her.

"The Devil has come to see us, Poppy. Don't slouch."

Cook would refuse to serve up a third plate, at first. She was a friendly, chirruping sort of thing, but she would not listen to the whims of my mother. She didn't want to encourage it, or so she would remark. Like most things, it began as unmentionable; Cook and I would exchange glances whilst my mother would sit and stare at the empty chair to her left. Then came the muttering. Cook would either exit the room, or raise her voice, in the hope of drowning out the unfathomable dialogue.

We would sit together, in our reading room, late into the evenings, trying to read or feign a game of something. My mother always loved games, of the board variety, my father hadn't been so keen on Hide and Seek in the house. Come to think of it, he was never so keen on anything that would reduce my mother to those old, familiar shrieks of laughter I had so begun to miss. She didn't play games anymore. She didn't shriek with laughter when I tried to catch her out anymore. She sat, quietly, wasting and unravelling and waiting for The Devil.

"Why has He come to see you, Mama?"

"Well, He hasn't told me." was her reply, short, sharp.

I thought, if The Devil really was coming to see us, perhaps it wasn't to see my mother at all, perhaps it was for the dumplings. I didn't suppose for a second that they had dumplings in Hell. I told her this, but she didn't think it very funny.

"Has He come for you, Mama?" I didn't want The Devil to take my mother just yet, I wanted to hear her laughter again, I wanted her to be here for just a little longer.

109

"I think He may have, Poppy." She was almost silent under the dim light of the reading lamps, the humidity outside still cloaking our house with sweat and discomfort. "Please tell Cook to keep all the windows open."

Just as quickly as she spoke, she left the room, wandering the hallways before drifting off to her bed. I would still hear her long into the night, restless, creaking across floorboards, faint whispers in the pitch black. Muttering to Him.

And one night, when Cook had read to me and the reading lamps had burned to their last, when my mother had ceased to patrol the hallway for the night, in her usual, nervous manner that I had become so accustomed to, when I had lain awake, having anxiously discarded sheep for counting the number of loose curls on my mother's head, when the heavy clouds that had hung so low over our house that summer erupted into two long nights of cool, soothing showers, I heard a single grunt in my left ear, a deep, guttural noise that startled me to an upright position in my bed. That was the night The Devil spoke to me.

The pitch black of my bedroom remained His hiding place for the night, He didn't exist as one entity, not at first. I heard His first grunt right beside my left ear, that evening. But, as I sat up, huddling my bedclothes around me, I could hear Him echoing from every corner of the room. My already pitch-black room seemed to darken, somehow, in his presence; I imagined Him as a wisp of black smoke, darting, shooting down the chimney, flitting between the dark spaces in my room. *Grunt.* He was here. *Grunt.* He was powerful. *Grunt.* My mother was not lying. *Grunt.* I didn't want Him to take her. *Grunt.* Not just yet.

I Have Come.

I didn't hear His words, but I felt them, vibrating through me as His wisp-like shadow darted across my table tops and bookcases, racing through my mind. I tried to speak to Him, I tried to ask Him what he wanted with us, with my mother, but my mouth was frozen into one perfect 'O', I could form no words, nor could I react to Him. I stared across at the wall, allowing Him to envelop my tiny figure, my eyes adjusting to his changeable silhouette. He repeated the same three words, words from the invisible mouth of His dancing shadow. I Have

110

Come. *Grunt.* I Have Come. *Grunt.* It was that same guttural sound, the words barely audible, blending together into a forced sentence. And just as quickly as He had startled me into waking, He disappeared again. No fading thoughts or threats, no muttering, He had come to see me and now He was gone. I shuddered, still unable to form words, as I sat huddled in the middle of my bed for what seemed like the longest and darkest of hours.

And that night, I dreamt of being pulled by long, wispy shadows across my bedroom floor, their ethereal fingers wrapping round my hair, like smoky tendrils, I felt their inhuman weight dragging me towards the fireplace, transparent in the moonlight, as my dream-body fought their flailing arms. I could hear the sounds of my mother running along the hallway, shrieking. I felt my body growing heavy, as the eerie tendrils dragged me ever closer to the fireplace, succumbing to the cold stone of the ground, to the unintended journey I was being forced toward. It was as if He was summoning me through dreams. I thought that perhaps my mother had been summoned also, that she may have felt His presence flitting across her as she slept, that the same curling tendrils that haunted my dreams had reached for her also. I thought about The Devil for a long time after that; I thought that perhaps it was me that He wanted after all.

***

September came and left in a whirl of heavy winds and constant rainfall. The heavens had opened, leaving no trace of the dense summer we had enjoyed. Long forgotten were the memories of lazy days lying in the garden, pestering John to help with his chores, the sense of freedom that came with a long, hot summer. I cherished the open windows, the breeze dancing with our net curtains, the lighter evenings that turned just as my mother started her habitual muttering, just as the third place was laid at our dining table. Now, it seemed, each and every room of my old, familiar house was shrouded in secrets, I had heard The Devil that night, in between counting curls and dreaming of shadows and I was waiting for Him to return. He shied away from our house that September, but I was terrified of His return.

It was difficult to rattle around in a large, empty house with nothing but reading hours and mealtimes for a routine. There were sums to do and sentences to write and little bits of history allotted to each day. My mother had long since forgotten to school me, so it came down to Cook to encourage the continuation of my studies. Cook's character was typical of her given station in our house: friendly, a little chubby round the edges and with barely any education to her name. If it wasn't for my adoration of her food, her stories and her affection, I would never have been able to lend my concentration to her stuttered tutoring. Each subject was half-read from a wealth of textbooks and taught with love. I think Cook was beginning to look upon me as a neglected child, what with my mother spending more and more time in her bedroom, away from us. The only time she ever appeared was for the evening meal, it became the single most enjoyable event of each passing day, I was near my mother, even if she was so finely tuned into our invisible guest and His empty place at our table. Just to be near to her was enough, I was afraid I would start to forget her, her curls, now a wiry mass cascading down around her shrinking shoulders. I wanted to remember her eyes: hazel, almost set in stone against her ivory skin, now sallow with the lack of sunlight, cheekbones that used to skim the delicate blush of her cheeks, now gaunt and jutting. I wanted to be near my mother, but seeing her made me feel uncomfortable.

Cook had called the doctor out several times that month, she complained of the rain, of the damp days that my mother spent wallowing in her bedroom, muttering, barely acknowledging my presence or the presence of anyone around her. I was ushered out of the room every time the doctor came to see her, too young for that sort of thing, I suppose. Though, at thirteen, I sometimes felt as if I knew more truths about my mother than the adults who were fussing around her, not truly seeing the signs. He *had* come. I imagined the doctor had poked and prodded my mother, whilst she lay there in a daze. I did not want to see that, anyway, I was glad to be out of the room. The doctor blamed the rain, of course, and the lack of sunlight. He thought she had a particularly severe case of influenza for a few days, but could find no extreme temperature, so I decided to tell him about The Devil, because clearly, in my mind, Cook had forgotten.

"Now, Poppy," said the doctor, he was most kindly, but patronising. "What you think your mother is seeing, are purely hallucinations. A bad case of what your mother may have, can sometimes cause people to see things that really aren't there at all."

I supposed that the doctor hadn't ever had a dream about smoky tendrils dragging him to Hell through his fireplace, nor had he been kept awake by a strange, inhuman grunting, nor watched as his mother had been reduced to nothing more than a muttering shell. I guessed that he would not understand, why would anybody understand the shadows that had been so forcibly and inexplicably cast over our home since that deep, heady summer?

Cook continued to clean around the house and provide our meals in the same frenzied way that she always had, only now with added concern for my mother's deterioration, or more concern for the fact that nobody could seem to snap her out of it. 'Twas all in the mind,' so she would say to me on the few occasions I had dared to raise it with her, a young girl need know nothing about the illnesses of the mind, nor the demons, so she thought, which made it harder for me to voice my fears about these tragic changes. John was a little more understanding, though still attempted a stiff attitude to my worries. There were things and places that even the mind couldn't make sense of, he would tell me, so we had to try not to understand it, but to comfort and encourage my mother back into her old, familiar daily routine. Cook assumed my mother would snap out of it, John was guarded, but I could tell there was more to him that just what he said. In the end, it was Cook who was first to flee from the fear induced by The Devil.

* * *

The night Cook fled our house prevails over my memory, as clear as if it were yesterday. As I said when I began my tale, I don't remember how it started, or even how The Devil's reign on our family came to its conclusion, but when Cook went, it left a scar most vivid. I can still recall the atmosphere spreading between the rooms, the faraway shrieks from our most stoic of employees. I think it stayed with me because I never thought she would be the first to succumb. Because I never thought she would leave me.

After a period of waiting for Him, a sign of Him, a sound, I felt the house start to take on a life of its own. There was no flying crockery, there were no phantom footsteps; but it was as if the house had found its own breath, you never felt quite...alone. It was as if The Devil had ensconced Himself in our walls, within our rooms, always lurking, invisible, a fleck at the corner of your eye. We were isolated in our house of shadows, watched by uninvited guests, but felt equally powerless to overcome Him.

In the weeks leading up to Cook's swift departure, my mother's behaviour had become stranger, she was no longer dressing for her trips downstairs for evening meals, preferring to swan into the dining room in her shabby nightgown, which hung loose around her frail body, its delicate satin dragging along the floor as she waltzed to a tune of her own. It was the mother we had lost when my father had left, only more intense, more comfortable in her state of separation from the rest of the world. I would no longer hear her pacing the floor at night, along the tiny hall that separated our two bedrooms, even her muttering had ceased. These changes were nothing but unnerving, I should have relaxed, felt more comfortable in her presence, but it felt like another part of her was simply…missing. It was as if my mother had come to accept herself as she now was, her muttering and fearfulness of whatever was engulfing her was fast disappearing, she was no longer afraid of Him or whatever had come to take her. She entered our dining room each night with an air of hopeful expectance, she carried herself with calm. I sat waiting for the day she would not waltz through the door at all. I wished it would never come.

My mother took her seat at our dining table, as usual, the middle seat between our invisible guest and myself. His place was set, as always, just in case He decided to make an appearance. I noticed that my mother would tread a little more carefully around His place, so as not to disturb the chair, the placemats, the atmosphere that had begun to hang around His dark, imposing place. As she sat down at the table, my mother looked at me, in the oddest of ways, I remember. Her head was facing downwards as her eyes slid towards mine, her mouth cracking into a smile most distorted, twisted, almost diagonal in its knowingness, piercing through me. And for the first time since she started disappearing, I sensed something evil in her. I looked away, straight down at the table, frightened.

Cook bustled into the dining room with two trays, breaking the uncomfortable silence with her usual mix of bubbling conversation and enthusiasm for the evening's meal that she had slaved over. John would always tuck into his portion, locked away in the kitchen quarters, refusing to eat in our dining room, no matter how many times I asked him and Cook to join me. I desired safety in numbers, I wanted the peace that their familiar faces brought, to face another human at His place, rather than the dread of an entity, an intruder I could neither see nor hear. It had occurred to me, over these last few, tense weeks just how much adults did not and could not see things that they did not want to. As much as my mother had succumbed to visions of her dark visitor, Cook and John had adopted a 'mind over matter' approach to the dishevelled, unrecognisable woman that my mother had become. I supposed that to share the dining table with us was to admit that there were forces at work, more frightening than we could have imagined. Their minds were closed to the happenings that were creeping in all around us, but I was both open to them and afraid of each and every step.

Within moments of Cook carefully placing our meal at the table, within seconds of me casting my eyes over a grateful plate of juicy meats and boiled potatoes, the room dimmed, for just a second. I glanced at the lights, all eight miniature braziers flickered, as if dimmed in unison, followed by a heavy gust of wind that blew through the core of the dining room, fluttering the weeks of unread newspapers as it howled.

I managed to steal a glance at Cook as she recovered from the sudden flicker, the gust that had propelled through our dining room.

"Must be a storm comin'," she said, smoothing down her apron as she placed the trays on the dining table.

I noticed her glance nervously at the windows, perhaps to check for openings or cracks, for an answer. I turned my head to face the windows, they were all shut tight, the night beyond them drawing in thick and fast, like black treacle. But it was cloudless and still, as still as any night. The three of us stayed silent, Cook contemplating the storm, my mother smiling at her plate and me, frightened at what had happened and what this could mean. And I swore, in the aftermath, locked deep into the walls of the house, that I could hear the faint sounds of a trot-trot-trotting, as The Devil made His winding way along our hallways to His place at our table.

Another flicker, this one longer, plunged the room into almost blackness, for a few seconds. Cook shrugged and flung a tea towel over her shoulder, her face a strange combination of fear and annoyance, as she made her way back to the sanctity of the kitchen area. I wanted to grab my plate and run after her, I wanted to eat my dinner in the safety of the kitchen. He was back, He was coming back.

I Have Come. *Grunt*

Then the strangest thing happened. Before Cook passed through the doorway that led from the dining room, she flew backwards across the room, as if attacked by an unseen force, crying out as she fell, full pelt, against the bookcase in a heap of flour dust and white overalls. She landed with a huge *thud,* her face as white as the apron she was wearing. We were not alone. For a few seconds, Cook just sat, staring at the doorway, numb to the muttering giggles of my mother, who remained unmoved and unnerved at the table. I followed Cook's gaze to the empty door, the last known place of the intruder who had pushed her aside in so brutal a manner, no human could force themselves against that shelving, Cook had indeed been pushed, by something unseen. She could not ignore the truths that were plaguing our house anymore.

Grunt. Grunt.

Cook raced to the kitchen without a backwards glance, leaving me to clear up the scattered papers and sit back down at the dining table next to my mother, who I noticed had removed three of the dumplings from her plate and placed them on the placemat in front of the third, sinister chair. But before I had time to register her behaviour, I was pulled to the kitchen by a loud shriek, the kind that would curdle even the thickest of blood.

Racing from the dining room to the kitchen, hardly conscious of leaving my mother to her own devices, I found Cook kneeling on the stone floor, head in hands. I shouted for her, running over to where she knelt, and placed a hand on her shoulder as I looked around for a culprit, a reason for her scream. I barely had time to notice the disarray that the kitchen was in, a pure state of chaos, with saucepans upturned on the stove and a huge sack of flour spilled over on the floor.

Cook stretched out a hand, leaving the other to cover her red, tear-stained face, as she pointed ahead of her. Following her hand, I found myself cowering behind my own as I saw what had startled her into such a frightened state. On the floor, beginning at the upturned flour bag and disappearing into the corner of the kitchen, almost to the back door, imprinted in flour and dirt, were the marks of a silent intruder. Short and stubby, these were not the prints of a man, nor a human of any description. They bore the unmistakeable marks of a hoofed creature.

I set about clearing up the spilled bag of flour, flurrying around Cook as she brought herself to standing, her clammy hand still clamped firmly around her mouth. I thought it would help to clear the evidence of The Devil's ransacking of her kitchen, but Cook seemed almost more startled by my efforts to clean. Once she had gathered what little thoughts she could muster and prised her hand away from her mouth, she took her leave and scurried to her bedroom. I heard little more from her, as I tidied the rest of the pots and pans, with help from John, who had been brought to the kitchen on hearing Cook's terrified screams. The last words I heard Cook utter were something about a 'hell house' as she stomped down the staircase, with a bag in hand and promptly left the building through the front door. She didn't give a backwards glance. With peace temporarily restored, my mother was still spooning bits of her dinner onto the empty placemat and I was trying my best to conceal the fear that was enveloping me.

Our home had always seemed a little imposing from the outside. The huge oak door with its long, heavy brass knocker towered above its residents and guests alike, whilst the whitewashed turrets on either side of the house were always visible from miles away. But it seemed all the more imposing without Cook. I felt such a surge of sadness when I returned from the village the following afternoon, walking up the gravel path with John, knowing that Cook's familiar, safe, ever-glowing face would no longer be there to greet us.

* * *

So the year began to wind down, in the midst of more silence and change, in our house anyway. September turned into a bitter October, the winds whistled, the rain continued to pour and The Devil continued to wreak His subtle, chaotic havoc, taking more and more pieces of my mother, who now enjoyed one-sided conversations over our dinners with her unseen guest. She would pour wine into a glass for Him, speak in muttered, unrecognisable tones as she played with her food. She became like a child play-acting with her dolls, always setting a place and a plate for our hoofed intruder, whilst John and I looked on in horror, when we could no longer simply hide in the kitchen. We felt helpless. The Devil had not made His presence known to us all, yet. I still supposed that He had crept in, through the back door, often left unlocked during those final silence-filled evenings at home. I supposed He had sidled past the scullery, the pantry door and the kitchen, where Cook no longer dwelt. His hooves must have clicked up the little stone steps, along the long hallway, as He made His way to our dining room table. I had still never seen Him, but I began to notice that His wine glass and plate were always empty.

With winter closing in swiftly, John had negated his gardening chores in order to help with the running of the house. Cook's absence had led us to simply shut up many of the rooms we didn't use. I had even taken to sleeping in our reading room, neglecting my bedroom for fear of staying too close to my mother, now almost unrecognisable with her dishevelled appearance, wafting from bedroom to dining room, never acknowledging John or I, there was nothing but quiet refusals to be parted from the house or from Him. So we did nothing, said nothing and waited for the inevitable return of The Devil. And that was the most terrible betrayal of all, when I look back upon those deep, isolating months now. We became too scared of what was going to happen next, we became too scared to acknowledge that we needed help. We even became too scared to admit that we were scared.

I had begun to realise that John only stayed because I did. I refused to leave what was left of my mother and so, in turn, he refused to leave me. He felt responsible and, even though The Devil had become part of life as we knew it, I felt safe with John and with that, I felt that we could keep my mother safe from the authorities that would be sure to take her from us. And so we stayed, as if under a spell, tutting at the small but insignificant nuisances that He caused around us, cutting ourselves off from others, muting our fears of what might happen next. We were existing from day to day in a haze of unfulfilled chores and unanswered questions. Not since Cook had He actually made an attack, but still He would leave subtle hints of His presence; more prints, upturned frames along the hallways, the clicking and grunting sounds that had become so intrinsic to daily life, ever since I had dreamt of his spectral slaves, dragging me to Hell. Life became numb and in the absence of anyone but each other, so did we.

Christmas was approaching, yet we had no reason for celebration this year. John took a rare trip to the local town to pick fresh Christmas wreaths with glossy, gold-tinged tartan ribbons, and sprigs of holly and fern to place around our empty fireplaces. But even in the depths of a snowy, picturesque winter, the decorations were lacklustre, dingy and out of place in the deafening atmosphere. There was not much at all to celebrate this year.

One day, shortly before December 25th, I asked John if we could cut down a small fir tree from the garden, a little one that rose just to my waist. I was in a strange mood for nostalgia, fleeting as it was, and I wanted a Christmas tree to decorate my makeshift bedroom. John agreed that it would be a good idea to spread a little cheer in a house that had become so cheerless, so we ventured out to the garden, under the watchful eye of my vacant mother, who stared at us from the self-imposed prison of her bedroom, three floors up. John fetched his axe, which had been left to rust in his potting shed and we made our way to a little grove of dwarf fir trees at the bottom of the garden.

I chose the tree I wanted, the littlest and, perhaps, most feeble of the grove, nestled in at the very end. John, visibly shaking from the cold of the snowy trunk he touched, bent down to start chopping. I saw him shivering as he held the axe in place, so I offered to run into the house and fetch some gloves.

"My gardening gloves are in the shed, Poppy." John replied, his ruddy complexion glowing against the white of the winter. "Woollen gloves would be awful slippery for this kind of work. Run along and find them, would you?"

I ran across to the potting shed to fetch John's gloves. Opening the shed door, I fumbled through various tools and pots, until I found a pair of stiff, green gloves that may well have been lying there for months. John's shed was not the tidiest of places, bits and pieces were shoved here and there, with every intention of being organised, I was sure. I started to climb over discarded planks of wood and large stone ornaments to grab the gloves for John, when I was suddenly stopped in my tracks by the sound of a long, deafening scream.

Racing back towards the trees, I was terrified of what I might find. I had fled the confines of the potting shed, not even stopping to shut the door. When I reached the little grove, the trees were still sat, as silent as they were, waiting for the next snowfall. I tiptoed around the grove, calling John's name, not giving a second thought to who else might be there. A rustle in the grove opposite made me jump, as a small bird shot into view, flitting along the top branches of a tree. I spotted a long, thin trickle of crimson sinking steadily into the snow. Not wanting to, but powerless to resist following the trickle with my eyes, it led to the most sorry and terrible sight my young eyes had ever seen.

Dear, sweet John was lying on the ground, his hands turning a certain shade of grey from the cold, his ashen face brushed on one cheek by a weeping fir and his axe firmly embedded in between the nape of his neck and the collar of his thick gardening coat. I screamed, for what seemed like hours, staying a clear distance from the body and from whatever evil had caused this hideous murder. Then I turned and ran back to the house, not stopping to wipe the streams of tears running down my face, nor acknowledge my mother's vacant, twisted stare from the top window, knowing that she had witnessed this gruesome killing.

I locked myself in the reading room, red with rage, seething with hopelessness. I could do nothing with John's body, I could do nothing with my mother, I was encased in a house of hatred and death, and I was the only one left who could save her. Without thinking, I began to tear down the shimmering decorations John had adorned my makeshift room with, the tartan ribbons were ripped to shreds, the holly torn from its hangings by my bare and bleeding hands. If there was no John, there was no Christmas. And I sat, for three full days, in amongst piles of green and red, and cried for everything that we had lost and everything that would still come to be.

* * *

The last time The Devil came to dinner, I saw Him. His marks had led me to believe Him to be a huge creature with matted fur, something that would tower and loom over me in my deepest nightmares. In truth, He was nothing more than a shapeless wisp of smoke that glided into our dining room and announced His presence with grunted commands. I heard the echoes of His smoke-hooves move through the house, there was no Cook, nor John, who would now be buried under smattering upon smattering of snowfall, to see Him this time. Through the back door left inexplicably ajar, past the scullery, past the pantry door, the kitchen empty with unnatural silence, I heard Him skipping up the stone steps, thudding through the hallway, but I stayed put on my dining chair. My mother, thinner than ever, her nightdress hanging from her shoulders, could barely stand to welcome Him.

"The Devil has come to see us, Poppy."

I didn't slouch, nor did I register that my mother had used my name, for perhaps the first time in months. I had passed the point of fear, Cook had fled, John had been killed and my mother had nobody but me to coax her back to the land of the living. I had been made all too aware of the horrors that could await my mother if she fell into the hands of the doctors, so I had taken it upon myself to stay with her, just until she was better, or until The Devil stopped visiting. There was a certain sense of contentment in the dreadful solitude that I had become used to. Most had abandoned my mother in the wake of her possession, I saw no need to leave now. Perhaps we would die here together.

The familiar scrapings of hoofed footsteps started along our empty hallway, the whispers of a wind that blew through the house, He was coming. My mother's twisted smile distorted into a grimacing laugh in anticipation of His arrival. She held her wine glass in one hand, as she tried to push herself up from the chair, her skeletal frame almost buckling under its own weightlessness. The dining room grew colder as He made His way through, the walls seemed to shift, to move as His very essence, His wisp, made its way to our dining table. I could make out no features, but I could feel I was being watched, I could make out no words, but I could feel Him trying to talk to me. My mother laughed, hysterically, clutching her wine glass as she sank back down onto the chair, her bony hand reaching out towards our translucent visitor. And with that moment of terrifying and wondrous clarity, came a sharp banging on the window behind me.

A face, white and distorted against the panes, shouted to me. I panicked at first, standing to attention as the voice broke our strange and sinister silence.

"Poppy!" the stranger shouted repeatedly, banging on the window.

Looking again, I saw it was the face of one of the local policemen. He was banging his truncheon on the window, my mother kept her back to him, bending her head into her chest, her laughter turning to weeping. All at once, our unwanted guest seemed to lose His grip on us, on the house. My flesh no longer crept with tingles of His presence, I could no longer make out the almost transparent shifts in His movements. The policeman was another human being, alive and here to help us and take us from Him. The face at the window, the banging that panicked me back to reality, it became these touches of humanity that brought me back to the living, but my mother wasn't allowed to come with me. My last memory of that evening was seeing my mother's tiny frame being bundled into the back of a police car. She didn't look back once, like Cook had also done, as the car sped off into the night, to deal her the most undeserved of fates.

I was taken away shortly after my mother, bundled into a car also and sped away with little time to pack or even think. With no-one to watch over me, it was decided by Cook who, upon hearing the news of John's death and my mother's forced departure, wrote to apologise for her sudden leaving and to assure me that she had arranged for me to be sent to my aunt for the foreseeable future. I had taken up residence with John's sister who, it seemed, I was to thank for sending the policeman out to save us. She had become worried about John after his notable silence over Christmas time, I supposed her fears were never quite as bad as the reality of John's death. She was hospitable towards me, as I was shoved on her doorstep the morning after our rescue, if a little wary of who I was and how much of her brother's death I had come to know. I stayed with John's sister for a full fortnight, until it was decided that I should be sent as far away from my home as I could be.

My aunt wrote to me, excitedly, after a few days, anxious for my arrival and keen to enrol me at a local school with my cousins. She lived in a cottage, in rural surroundings about two hours from my former home, with her husband and two children, both of whom were of a similar age to me. She wrote that I was to have a bed placed in my cousin Annette's bedroom, and that they were looking forward to seeing me. I should have been glad to be given the opportunity to start anew. I should have been glad to see the back of those last few seasons, but my departure was bittersweet, for though I was safe and my mother had been taken to a much safer place also, I couldn't shake the feeling that I had somehow let her down. We did all we could to protect her from those who would keep her locked up, submit her mind and body to all sorts of intrusive exercises. So perhaps, despite all my efforts, I had my freedom, and my mother was sentenced to twenty years incarceration in a correctional facility, upon an assumed guilty plea to John's murder. In many ways, I still felt I had failed her.

* * *

I turn sixteen next week, I suppose there will be a Victoria sponge cake and tea served in the 'special china' to celebrate. Annette turns sixteen just under a month later too. The last few years have been somewhat strained, settling into a new way of life and schooling under the permanent, oppressive supervision of an aunt who loves and cares for me, to the point of emotional asphyxiation. Often, it is not what she says as much as the gaps in between our conversations, the things she won't mention. She has always made a stark choice not to talk about the events that led up to my mother's incarceration, preferring to wonder and marvel at how 'normal' a girl I've grown into, all things considered.

I have only been to visit my mother once, under the supervision of my uncle, who stood in the corner glaring at my mother as she sat and asked polite questions, stopping only to sip on a small glass of water, before she was herded back to the correction unit by a cumbersome nurse. I write to her almost every week with tales of school and summer, about my cousin's insistence on enlisting with the army and all that is going on in the outside world. I write to her as I would talk to her, omitting any kind of emotion, just as she seemed unable to show any to me on my one permitted visit. The Devil took so many pieces of her, tormented her, a willing victim, for months and she has never fully recovered. I am no longer under any illusion that she will.

I dreamt of my mother last night, for the first time in weeks. I often dream of her in that once familiar, contorted, twisted shell that she had become. She never speaks to me, she beckons to me, encourages me to follow her along twisted maze-like pathways, spirals with no ends, she becomes a living, breathing version of those creatures who tried to drag me to Hell all that time ago, in that house, to that fireplace. This dream was different though, rather than following the back of her head, she was running towards me, from a distance. She looked to be smiling, there was a glimpse of all that was before The Devil. But as she got closer, and I remained glued to the spot, as I so often found myself in dreams, I watched as her face began to contort, to slide, the corners of her mouth pointed upwards, revealing jagged, vile teeth.

I jerked awake, the vision of my mother's monstrous face blurring into memory as I sat up in bed. I fumbled for the bedside light, willing to see something familiar again, even to hear Annette's soft breathing as she slept. I heard nothing, the house remained still, quiet, undisturbed.

But somewhere, from outside, or perhaps deeper inside these walls, I thought I could hear the faint sound of a trot. *Trot. Trot.* A creeping trot, He would click up the little stone steps and make his way through the front door. *Trot, trot, trot.* And every time, He would get a little bit closer.

Trot

Trot

Trot

The Devil has come to see you, Poppy.

Don't Slouch.

PEACH BERRY

ABOUT THE AUTHOR

Peach Berry is a qualified hair and make up artist by day and weaver of gothic fiction by night. Her fascination with ghost stories started at a very early age, when she would save up her pocket money to buy books about the paranormal and conduct ghost hunts at her primary school. She cites the work of Susan Hill, Stephen King and James Herbert as some of her biggest writing influences, though it doesn't hurt to be a die-hard heavy metal fan too!

Peach hails from the wilds of Somerset originally, but now resides in Nottingham with her daughter.

PEACH BERRY

Other Authors With Green Cat Books

Lisa J Rivers –

Why I have So Many Cats

Winding Down

Searching (Coming 2018)

Luna Felis –

Life Well Lived

Gabriel Eziorobo –

Words Of My Mouth

The Brain Behind Freelance Writing

Mike Herring –

Nature Boy

Glyn Roberts & David Smith –

Prince Porrig And The Calamitous Carbuncle

(other Prince Porrig books to follow)

Coming Soon With Green Cat Books

Elijah Barns –

The Witch and Jet Splinters: Part 1. A Bustle In The Hedgerow

Michelle DuVal -

The Coach

Sean Gaughan –

And God For His Own

David Rollins –

Haiku From The Asylum

ARE YOU A WRITER?

We are looking for writers to send in their manuscripts.

If you would like to submit your work, please send a small sample to

books@green-cat.co

GREEN CAT BOOKS

www.green-cat.co/books